STORMY SUMMER

SUZY TURNER

Stormy Summer
by Suzy Turner

Copyright 2015 Suzy Turner
The characters and events portrayed
in this book are fictitious.
Any similarity to real persons, living or dead,
is coincidental and not intended by the author.
All rights reserved. No part of this publication may be reproduced, distributed, or
transmitted in any form or by any means, or stored in a database or retrieval system,
without the prior written permission of the author.

Find out more information about Suzy's books at www.suzyturner.com

CHAPTER 1

I was having the time of my life. It was like being on a roller coaster of physical sensations. This guy was taking me to heaven and back. Touching me in all the right spots and taking me to the edge, over and over and over again. He was gentle and tender and not once did he ask me to do anything peculiar to him—as was often the case in my traumatic love life. Mmmmm, gosh it was good. He was amazing. Perhaps he was some kind of tantric sex expert, like Sting, because it seemed to go on for hours and hours. Believe me, this was one sexual experience I never wanted to end.

After a little while longer, I was right on the verge of having the most awesome orgasm of my entire life (it was definitely going to be more than multiple), when the inevitable happened: the phone started ringing. Shit. I told him to ignore it, and he did. But for some obscure reason, I couldn't. Suddenly, he wasn't there anymore. He seemed to have vanished into thin air. What the...?

Then it hit me like a left jab from Muhammad Ali. It wasn't the phone at all—it was the fucking alarm clock! Oh no, I was right there. Nearly there. Goddammit it. The bloody alarm clock was waking me from the most glorious dream of all time. I leant over the bedside table and switched the stupid thing off.

Still feeling incredibly horny and totally frustrated, I simply had to do something about it.

It was times like these that I needed a man. A real man, not some imaginary one.

So I reached under the bed and pulled out the 'joke' present Gwen had bought me for my birthday—an intimate massager. That's what it said on the box, anyway. Why didn't it just say 'Vibrator—for the sad, manless woman who needs it after an arduous night of dreamed up passion, rudely interrupted by the alarm clock'?

I switched it on. Nothing. Shit. By this time, I was desperate to fulfil myself where the alarm had prevented the dream from succeeding.

The batteries had run out. Instead, I used the ones from the alarm, tossing the clock onto the floor. I tried again, and it almost jumped out of my hand. That was more like it.

Carefully placing the buzzing piece of equipment between my legs, I tried to fantasise about the hunk in the dream. But I just couldn't picture him, so I settled for Russell Crowe instead. Mmmmm, yeah, Russell, baby, yeah. Hang on a minute, that wasn't Russell. It was... it was... it was bloody Austin Powers! What on Earth was wrong with me? Not that it particularly mattered, because within a couple of minutes (after turning up the power) I'd finally managed to come (even though I'd been imagining having sex with a total geek, not a god. Never mind). And it wasn't quite the same standard as before—just a short single one; orgasm, that is. At least I'd got rid of the need. I wished I had a real man. And I wished I could figure out who the sexy beast in my dream was.

I didn't have the slightest idea who I'd been fantasising about. And boy...what a fantasy. It would probably come to me when I was thinking of something completely different. Like when I was at work, amidst the countless dorks in the office, or somewhere irritating like that.

Finally climbing out of bed and wondering what time it was, since I'd nicked the batteries from the clock, I decided to get a move on. I couldn't be late for work. Otherwise, Mr Negativity would hit the roof. He usually did.

oOo

As I INCHED FORWARD in the traffic jam, I noticed I was being ogled by a couple of rather fat, ugly, perverted builders. You know the kind—builders' bum cracks and all.

They were crudely suggesting a 'shag' and grabbing their crotches and stuff. I gave them the finger and mouthed 'sit, and spin, gentlemen' before the traffic finally began to speed up and off I went.

Only another five minutes and I'd be pulling up outside The News Corporation, the gigantic office building near London where I worked. It was quite an impressive place. The only one of its kind in England. We also had a sister building in New York, and another in Texas.

Over here, it was a multi-storey office block, where several daily, weekly and monthly newspapers and magazines were created.

I worked at the Monthly News Gazette, where I was responsible for page-making, as well as a few other boring bits and bobs. The page-making could be quite a bit of fun sometimes; just a shame about the rest of it, really.

My boss was Jack Willoughby, aka Mr Negativity. The single most negative person ever to exist this side of Mars. Nothing was ever right; his problems were the only problems in the world. He was always talking about moving abroad because he couldn't stand the weather, as well as countless other stuff. Basically, he was a right pain in the arse.

There were hundreds of staff and, for some reason, my department seemed to have all the geeks and tarts. I seemed to be the only real normal person there—at least I thought I was normal, anyway. Well, relatively normal.

As I finally pulled into the car park, I suddenly had a massive flashback, and I finally saw the guy from my dream. It was... It was... OH MY GOD! I was so shocked that I braked too late and shunted a parked car. Shit. I glanced around to see if there were any witnesses, but luckily there didn't seem to be anyone around. So I quickly parked away from the other vehicle. I turned off the engine and just sat there in shock—not because I had driven into another person's car, but because of the dream. Or should I say nightmare? The tantric sex god had been none other than the fat office slob, Gavin Knobb.

I couldn't bear the thought. I shuddered, trying to force it from my mind. Urgh. I was totally and completely grossed out. I couldn't tell anyone, not even Gwen. Okay, yeah, I could tell Gwen; she was my best pal. I'd tell her all the disgustingly gruesome details tonight. It was funny how just a couple of hours earlier, these details were blissfully delightful, and now they were totally gross.

I went and had a look at the other car to see if I'd damaged it. I had...but only a little. Well, it didn't look that bad. Oh, fucking hell! Feeling totally guilty, I figured I'd better scribble down a note with my apologies and phone number. I put it under the wiper and then headed into work.

It was exactly 08h30. Right on time.

'On-time this morning, for a change, Summer,' quipped possibly the geekiest of them all, Geoff Wankhorn, as he handed over some news articles on a flash drive, ready to be transformed into an interesting page that people would want to read.

'Oh, bugger off, Wanker.'

Of course, he hated being called that, but it was the best way to get him to shut up, and almost everyone in the office used it at some point or other. I must admit, though, that I did feel sorry for him sometimes (and I stress sometimes) but today wasn't one of those days. After this morning's palaver, everyone was in my bad books—particularly Gavin the Knobster (as I often called him) for managing to creep into my dream like that. How dare he, for God's sake! Urgh! Urgh! Urgh! I quivered all over in disgust.

Think of the devil, and he shall appear. Bollocks.

There he stood, waiting for me at my desk. I stopped in my tracks and eyed him from a distance. He really was horrible. Quite tall but fat, and he wore trousers so tight they almost tore at the seams and a baggy brown cotton shirt with stains down the front.

His lanky brown hair needed a good cut and blowjob—erm, blow-dry (what was wrong with me?). Added to that was the disgusting fact that he obviously hadn't wiped his mouth after eating break-fast. How could I have possibly dreamt about having the best sex of my life with such a freak? I groaned, obviously aloud, because he looked up and saw me.

'Mornin', alright?' he slobbered.

Cringing, I nodded and asked if he was waiting for something.

'Well, yeah. I, er, I, I was wonderin' if you. Er...'

Oh God, what on Earth was he going to ask? He wasn't going to ask me out or something, was he? Please no.Please. Then, I had another thought. Oh God no—he didn't have the same dream, did he? No, no, no, no, no, no! Urgh! With a capital U. I couldn't bear it. I looked him straight in the eye, and that's when I noticed he actually had the most lovely emerald green eyes. Well, that's something I hadn't noticed before.

Suddenly I began to feel quite warm down there, in the groin area. Oh no—this was not happening—he was turning me on. No way. Oh, for God's sake, Summer, sort yourself out! Uh-oh. I didn't like the feel of this. Well, actually, I loved the feel of this, but just definitely and absolutely not with him.

He suddenly let out a loud burp and a faint odour of baked beans drifted beneath my nostrils. The warm feeling vanished. Thank God.

'Gavin, what is it? Just spit it out.' Not literally, though, I should have added.

'I lost quite an important file, and I was wondering if you'd seen it. It's the one about Kelly Brook's latest conquest.'

That's an important file? 'Why don't you ask Wanker?' I suggested, pointing behind me.

Finally, as I sat down to get some work done, Mr Negativity waltzed in. Okay, perhaps he didn't waltz in, because that would be a contradiction in terms. It would be far too positive a movement for him. He trundled in as if he had the world's problems at his feet. Oh, I forgot—he did have the world's problems at his feet, because his problems were the only problems in the world, right? Silly me for forgetting such an obvious thing.

As usual, I put my head down and avoided having to talk to him.

The worst thing you could do was to ask him how he was. Occasionally, if I were in a good mood, I'd forget and ask. Then my good mood would be gobbled up by the aura of negativity that surrounded him day and night—not that I'd ever seen him at night.

However, I couldn't avoid him forever as he was my boss, the editor of the Monthly News Gazette, and we had to liaise, rather too often for my liking, regarding the page make-up, articles, and so on.

Monday morning was often the worst because there was a pile of notes, messages, news clippings and complaints on his desk, as well as the fact that the Gazette was printed on the last Sunday of the month and the day before had been the printing day.

As if on cue, Willoughby picked up the latest edition and began his daily musings, or should I say moanings?

He tutted. 'Oh, for God's sake. Didn't I ask for someone to alter this headline? Summer? I do recall asking you to change it. Why hasn't it been done?'

'Well, Jack,'—we were all on a first-name basis—'I did change it, but then you asked to change it back again because it didn't sound quite right, if you recall,' I replied sweetly, with a hint of sarcasm, which was totally lost on him, I might add.

He muttered something to himself and turned his attention back to the magazine and yelled, 'Ricki, get me a coffee. White, three sweeteners, as usual.'

His young assistant curtseyed behind his back while the rest of us sniggered. Again, he missed it.

I watched Ricki in her tight pink mini skirt, high-heeled shoes, and virtually transparent blouse seductively sway her hips as she walked over to the coffee machine. She was wearing rather a lot of make-up, and her blonde shoulder-length shaggy hair was continually flicked in an attempt to look sexy. Considering the looks she was getting from the numerous dorks in the room, it obviously worked.

Personally, I thought she looked like a tart. Simple, really. Actually, Ricki was a bit on the simple side, and she was a bit of a tart.

Ricki's biggest admirer seemed to be Grayson Rosenblum, who was actually less of a dork than the rest. In fact, he was rather cute and, come to think of it, he had quite a sexy physique if perhaps a little skinny. Looking at him closely, he actually resembled Nicholas Cage (albeit very slightly). Jeeze... Why the hell had I never noticed him before?

I guess I'd never really taken any notice of the men in the office because I'd resigned myself to becoming celibate, especially since my relationship with Russell, which had ended when I found him in bed with my mother. That was one whole year ago, roughly around the time that I began working at the Gazette.

Believe me, finding the man intended to be the father of one's future children having sex with one's tart-of-a-mother was not a welcome or pretty sight.

I cried for about four months solid. If it hadn't been for Gwen's great support through the entire period, I'd probably still be sobbing away now, feeling sorry for myself and never wanting a relationship with another man again. In fact, if it weren't for Gwen, I'd probably be a lesbian by now.

I forgave my mother, but I couldn't forgive Russell. In fact, he never showed his face around town again. I'd heard that he'd shacked up with some blonde bimbo down in Devon somewhere. No big loss.

My mother had always been like that. A tart that is. And my father...well, I never knew him, because I was the result of a one-night stand some twenty-four years ago. I don't think my mum knew anything about him, either. I'd be surprised if she even knew his name.

I think that sad beginning to my life has had something to do with the fact that so far, my relationships with men have always ended terribly. Before Russell, there had been Aaron the biker, who only gave a shit about his bike. He was so obsessed with it that I hadn't been too surprised at finding him sitting naked on it in his garage while jerking off. I left him to it and didn't see him again. No big loss.

After my obscure dream, I guessed it was about time to try

again with men. I mean, for the past few months I've been having sex with something that requires batteries, for God's sake.

I had another look at Grayson, which turned into a long hungry stare. He caught me looking and smiled. I smiled back and blushed from head to toe. He was actually a bit of a hunk. At least he looked like a bit of a hunk. His problem was his fascination with the young, under-dressed, high-pitched little Ricki. I came to the conclusion that if he fancied her, then I was definitely not his type.

With my short-cropped blonde hair, tall sporty figure, small boobs, tendency to wear clothes that leave something to the imagination, and the ability to hold a decent conversation, I was probably exactly what he didn't like in a woman.

Oh well. Back to celibacy.

Suddenly bringing me crashing back down to reality, Mr Negativity was at it again, tutting some more. 'You know, I take one step forward and ten steps back in this place. Why hasn't this been done?' he hollered at one of the poor messengers from upstairs, as she quickly shrugged her shoulders and retreated back out of the main office.

'Bleeding moaner, why the hell can't he just leave everyone alone and take a long walk on a very short pier,' whispered Jim, a colleague who closely resembled an albino rabbit, with light ginger hair, freckly face, deathly white skin and constantly bloodshot eyes. It's no wonder he still lived at home with his mum, especially considering he was over 50 years old. He seemed like a nice bloke, though, but... ahem...definitely not my type. I nodded in agreement and decided to get some work done.

A few hours later, starving and ready for a bite to eat, I grabbed my handbag and headed outside into the rain. Deciding on a nice healthy lunch, I headed towards McDonald's. But before I got there, I felt something vibrating in my handbag. Pulling out my mobile, I put it to my ear.

'Hello?'

'Hello. Look I've just found your note on my car. Can we meet?' said the male voice on the other end of the line.

Shit.

'Sure, but I was just about to grab some lunch. Do you work at The News Corporation? If you do, perhaps we could meet there after work.'

'Yes I do, but I was just about to get some food too. Where are you now?'

Oh great, now I've got to sit down with some pompous arse stranger going on about their precious car for an hour when all I wanted was some peace and quiet and a decent bloody burger and a nice big strawberry milkshake.

'Sure. I was heading to McDonald's. I'll wait for you there. I'm quite tall with short blonde hair, and I'm wearing...'

'Black stockings and suspenders, I hope!' chuckled the voice.

I pretended to find him amusing and told him I was actually wearing a grey trouser suit with a pink blouse and I'd wait for him inside the entrance. What a perv.

A couple of minutes later, I felt a hand on my shoulder and turned to find Grayson staring back at me.

'Grayson, it's you!' I gasped.

'Well, you don't think I would have made the comment about stockings and suspenders to a complete stranger, do you?' he said with a warm smile.

'Yeah, but how did you know it was me?

'A friend in accounts saw it happen.'

'Oh. I'm really sorry about your car.'

'That's okay, we'll talk about it later. But first, food—I'm famished. How about you? Lunch is on me.'

'Don't be silly. It's on me, especially after I put a dent in your car.'

'Summer, I insist. Let me take a beautiful woman out for lunch.'

My smile faded. He'd brought Nicki with him. 'So where is she then?'

'I was talking about you, you silly girl,' he laughed as he steered me towards the queue. 'So, what do you fancy?'

Besides you, I thought, eyeing him up and down and picturing what he would look like lying in my bed... naked except for a bow tie.

I opted for the chicken nuggets: far less messy, and I could eat them looking a tad more seductive than if I were stuffing a mayonnaise-filled burger into my mouth.

We had a great lunch, talking about work and stuff, but I figured he wasn't really interested in me as he didn't really ask about me personally.

But as we were walking back to the office, he stuttered, 'Summer, I... Would you... Shall we...?' I concluded that perhaps he was asking me out on a date. Or rather, I hoped he was, anyway. I smiled, and finally, he came out with it. 'Would you like to go out with me sometime?'

'You know, Grayson, I'd love to,' I said, as he held open the office door for me.

Gosh, he was a real gentleman, too.

'How about Friday night? I'll come and pick you up,' he asked.

'That would be terrific. I'll give you my address later. And thanks for lunch. Oh, the car. You must let me pay for it.'

But he wouldn't accept anything.

Bloody hell, this really was turning into a good day, after all.

CHAPTER 2

When I arrived home later that afternoon, Gwen was waiting for me. She lived in the flat upstairs, so it wouldn't have mattered if I was late.

'Hello, Luv,' she said in her wonderful broad Yorkshire accent.

'Hiya. Did you just come downstairs?'

'Uh-huh. Literally. Look, I bought a bottle of wine! Okay, I bought two, and I made a chicken casserole. I'll be expecting you at seven on the dot. Okay, Luv?'

'Gwen, that sounds like heaven. Speaking of heaven, I've got a funny story to tell you, but I'll tell you all about it later. Do you want me to bring anything?'

'Just you and your funny story, Luv,' she said as she skipped up the stairs back to her place. 'See you in a bit!'

'Okay, bye!'

oOo

'...AND then I was in such a state that I hit a car in the parking lot!'

By this stage, Gwen was rolling about on the floor in hysterics.

'No more, my stomach can't take it. Stop making me laugh, Summer!'

'You're not supposed to be laughing, you're supposed to be sympathetic—I dreamt I was having the best sex of my life with a total nob—literally—woke up before coming, had to use a blinking vibrator to finish off the job and then I go and crash my car, and you're in bloody hysterics! Some friend you are, Gwen Pursehouse!'

But by the time I'd finished, I was in fits of the giggles too. I mean, I guess it was pretty funny.

'I'm glad that you found a good use for your birthday present!' she guffawed.

'Ooh, yeah, what a great pressie. Ooh, yeah, baby yeah,' I said in my best Austin Powers impersonation.

Laughing, we began to clear the dining table after polishing off the remains of the delicious casserole that Gwen had created earlier.

'You know, Gwen, that casserole really was something else. It was absolutely delicious. No wonder Hugh wants to marry you.'

'Oh charming, you mean you're saying it's got nothing to do with my amazingly gorgeous looks and body and my personality-to-die-for?' she said, trying hard to look serious.

'You know what I mean, girl! So, why don't you take him up on his offer? He's a nice enough guy. Except for the fact that...'

'Don't say it, Summer... No, I said don't say it,' she said, her face screwed up in an attempt not to laugh.

'The fact that his name is Huge Johnson!' I burst into raucous laughter at the thought.

'His name is not Huge Johnson at all! It's Hugh Johnson! There's a difference. A huge difference! And stop laughing, you. Stop it, stop it.' She started flicking me with a rolled up dishcloth.

'Ouch! I'm sorry, but I just can't help it. It's so funny. I mean, come on, well... does Hugh Johnson have a huge johnson?' I laughed.

'Summer! As a matter of fact, he does, but don't tell him I told you so!'

'Lucky ol' you, girl!'

We laughed and finished washing the dishes and then went and sat down with a couple more glasses of wine.

'So what is the real deal with you and Hugh, then? He's asked you to marry him so many times. I'm beginning to feel quite sorry for him,' I asked.

'You don't marry someone just because you feel sorry for them, do you? Besides, I've told him I'm not ready for the marriage scene just yet. We're happy as we are, at the moment. We don't need some stupid piece of paper, do we?'

'Oh, come on, Gwen, you've got a weird thing going on with the guy. When you're feeling horny, you give him a call. Otherwise, you don't bother. And the fact that he's willing to wait around for you like that is incredibly sweet. He obviously really loves you.'

'Oh, for God's sake, Summer, I don't want to talk about it anymore, okay? Please just give me a break,' she snapped.

I apologised for being so pushy, realising that it was obviously a bit of a sore point. I wondered why but left it at that, so I changed the subject by telling her about the rest of my day.

'I still haven't told you about my peculiar lunch hour today,' I stopped for a swig of wine and continued, 'and I managed to get a date with rather a nice looking chap from work. We're going out on Friday night.'

'Bloody hell, Summer, that's big—like real big—news. Why didn't you tell me when you first arrived? So who is he, then?'

'His name is Grayson Rosenblum, and he works at the Gazette. Actually, it was his car that I shunted.'

'You're joking,' she said in awe.

I shook my head. 'I put a note on his windscreen, not knowing that it belonged to him, and he called me up at lunchtime. We ended up having lunch—on him—and he wouldn't let me pay for the damage to his car. Mind you, it was only a little dent, and then he asked me out, and I said I'd love to. So we are. Going out, that is,' I explained.

'But I remember, once upon a time, when you told me that you'd never date anyone from work, remember?'

'Yeah, I know, but I reckon...' I stopped mid-speech, wondering whether to tell her or not, considering she'd only laugh. Oh, what the hell, 'I reckon my dream was a sign that I should try out some blokes from work!' There I said it.

'You what? You think your dream was a sign to shag anybody and everybody from work? Whoever you are, what have you done with the real Summer? I want her back, right now!' shouted Gwen, pretending she was surrounded by aliens or something.

'I'm not going to sleep with everyone from work!'

'Well, you've already slept with Gavin, and you're thinking of shagging this Grayson bloke. Right?'

'I have not shagged Gavin!' I said, feeling my face turning a weird crimson colour.

'Aha, but you didn't deny that you wanted to shag Grayson's brains out, did you?' Seeing the look on my face, Gwen softened, 'Oh honey, I'm sorry. I was just kiddin'. You're entitled to a bit of sexy fun, of course, you are. I'm just concerned, that's all. I know what offices can be like. If it doesn't work out with this bloke, yer know how people talk'.

'Yes, of course, I do, but I deserve to enjoy myself with a man for a change. After all, I haven't for a whole bloody year. I'm beginning to feel like a nun, for God's sake,' I said, crossing my body. 'Spectacles, Testicles, Wallet and Watch', we said in unison, laughing.

'Well, you enjoy him, then. But whatever you do, don't shag Mr Negativity!'

'Urgh, ooh! Gross!' I yelled as I threw a cushion at her in disgust.

'Watch the wine, watch the wine,' she shrieked.

'Does this mean that you give my little plan your blessing?'

'Of course! I'm behind yer all the way, girl. Just don't forget to give me all the little details. I hope this Grayson bloke is everything you've ever wanted in a man, and then you won't have to be tempted by the countless hunks—not—who work with you, will you?' she said.

I agreed, hoping she was right. 'Shall we open that other bottle of wine and watch a movie? What do you think? Dirty Dancing okay with you?'

'You always pick that one.'

'I wonder why! Patrick Swayze is such a hunk, and I want to be Jennifer Grey!' I swooned.

'Okay, good point. Very good point. Dirty Dancing it is,'

CHAPTER 3

The rest of the week went by relatively smoothly, the only problems were with Mr Negativity. On Thursday his ex-wife paid him a visit; not a good thing, as this meant he'd be in a particularly bad mood for the rest of the day, and the next day, and probably the next week, too.

Well, I didn't care, I was in a good mood and even he wasn't going to screw that up.

Grayson and I had spoken very little to each other, probably because we didn't want people to talk, plus we'd had a lot of work to do. He was only in the office for a couple of hours a day, as he was a reporter and photographer, so he was out reasonably regularly on stories. I made a point of seeing him on Friday morning to give him my address and make sure the date was still on.

'Good morning, Summer. How are you? I hope Willoughby isn't giving you too much hassle?' he asked in his smooth posh accent.

'I'm great, thanks. Mr Negativity over there is easy enough for me to handle. So, are we still on for tonight?'

'Of course. Can I have your address?'

I handed it to him. Our hands touched briefly for the first time, which made me gasp slightly. By the way, he looked at me, he obviously noticed. I went somewhat red and grinned.

'I'll pick you up at 07h30. Is that okay with you?'

'That'll be great. I'll see you then.'

He picked up his photography gear and headed out of the office, looking back once to nod his head and smile at me.

Unfortunately, Wankhorn and Gavin the nobster had noticed our brief 'meeting', and both made pathetic remarks.

I ignored them and tried to get some work done. However, it was a lot easier said than done, considering Mr Negativity's visit the day before and his increasingly annoying fits of coughing. A smoker's cough, too, I might add.

'Christ. Can't anyone get it right?' he shouted from his desk. 'Summer. Come here. You've done it again!'

I rolled my eyes backwards and went to see what I'd done wrong this time.

As it turned out, I hadn't done anything wrong; it was his fault, again. He'd made a spelling mistake and, as usual, was quick to blame everyone else for his little fuck-ups.

'Yes, Jack, no, Jack. Three bags full, Jack,' I whispered as I went back to my desk.

'If anybody wants me, I'll be outside,' he said, with some mention of a fag break, which was probably his twentieth that day.

When he came back, he was coughing his guts up once again. 'I really must get the doctor to check this out,' he muttered as he walked past.

'Stop smoking and the cough will quit, you silly arse,' said someone from the back of the office.

He chose to ignore the comment, knowing they were right, but not keen to acknowledge anybody else's intelligence over his. 'I don't want to be interrupted for the next couple of hours, everybody. I have a great deal of work to do,' he announced.

Again somebody stated the obvious, 'You wouldn't be so busy if you stopped taking so many bloody fag breaks.'

He eyed his staff to see who'd made the comment and then realised he didn't have a decent retort, so he gave up.

At last, it was five o'clock and I was the first out of the office. I needed as much time as possible to get ready for my date.

'Enjoy your little date, Summer. Summer and Grayson sitting in a tree, K-I-S-S-I-N-G...' sang Gavin and Geoff.

'Give it a break, you two. You're just jealous!' I said as I walked out of the door without a single glance back. Prats.

oOo

GWEN HAD AGREED to help me choose what to wear so, as usual, she was waiting for me at my front door.

'Hello, you. Excited, are you?'

'Extremely. And I stopped at the off-licence to pick up a bottle of wine so we could have a glass while I got ready'.

'Super idea, luv.'

We walked into my flat and Gwen put on some groovy music while I poured the wine.

'Here you go. I'm just going to pop into the shower. Come in and chat?'

We took our wine into the bathroom. Gwen sat herself down on the loo while I undressed and stepped under the blissfully hot water.

'So, are you seeing Hugh tonight?' I asked from behind the shower curtain.

'Yep. He's comin' round at eight-ish. Bringing pizza with him. And wine.'

'So, yet another night of unbridled passion with the huge one, is it?'

'It certainly is,' she giggled.

'You're so lucky. Pass me the shower gel, please. Thanks.'

I leaned out of the shower to have a quick swig of wine, then washed my hair and shaved everywhere that needed it. And believe me—it needed it.

'I take it you're planning on getting laid tonight, then?' Gwen asked, pointing to the fact that I'd just made sure I was hairless in all the right places.

'No, I don't think so. It's a bit too soon. Not on a first date. That would make me a bit of a tart, wouldn't it? I don't particularly want that kind of label.' I thought about it some more. 'Actually, Gwen, sod it. I'm feeling really horny, and if we hit it off, then I'm more than happy to get laid tonight,' I said with a satisfied smile as the two of us clinked wine glasses. 'Here's to a great lay.'

'Hear, hear!' she answered.

In my bedroom (which I'd cleaned particularly well the night before - just in case), Gwen and I went through my wardrobe, trying to find something suitable to wear.

'So, do you know where you're going?'

'Not a clue.'

'Shit, then. Okay, well you're pretty restricted with the weather. It's bloody cold outside, so you'd be better off wearing your boots,' Gwen commented as she pulled out my favourite boots from the bottom of the cupboard.

'Okay, so I wear my sexy high-heeled knee-high black suede boots and nothing else,' I said, putting the boots on, dropping the towel and doing a twirl.

'Well, if I were a man, I'd have a major hard-on!' laughed Gwen.

'Well, thank you, kind sir. You've made my day.'

Together, we decided on a simple tight black knee-length dress with long flared sleeves. Beneath it, I decided to be really naughty and wear absolutely nothing except for hold-up-stockings. I wore black mascara, grey eye shadow, a little blusher and pale pink lipstick. Gwen did my hair, just-fell-out-of-bed style. I must admit I looked good. In fact, I was so pleased with the result that we decided to have another glass of wine to celebrate the new sexual me.

At precisely 7.30, there was a knock at the door. It was Grayson.

'Wow! You look gorgeous, Summer.' He'd brought a big bunch of carnations (not exactly my favourite, but I guess he wasn't to know that), which was a lovely thought.

Gwen was just about to leave, so I introduced the two. She winked at me as she left, whispering, 'Go, girl.'

'Would you like a glass of wine before we go out?' I asked.

'Why not? Just a small one, thanks.'

I poured us both a glass of red, and we sat down in the living room.

'This is a nice place you've got here. Have you been here long?'

'About five years now. I love it. It's home. What about you? Where do you live?'

'A couple of blocks away from here, on Clifton Avenue. I rent a small flat down there.'

'Yeah, I know the area. Actually, my mum lives fairly close.'

I handed him a small dish of black olives. 'Help yourself. I realise they're not everyone's cup of tea, but I love them.'

'I agree, olives are definitely an acquired taste, but once acquired, you can't get enough of them. So you're a fan of Mediterranean food, are you?' he asked.

'I love it. Mind you, I like most foreign food. English stuff is a bit bland if you ask me. Although my friend Gwen—the girl you just met, she's a great cook. She can make anything, and everything tastes delicious. Unfortunately, though, I'm not so great at it. I prefer to stick to pasta and stuff like that. Simple but tasty.'

'Well you sure are fabulous at pouring a glass of wine and putting olives in a bowl,' he commented with a wide grin.

Gosh, he really was handsome—but in a slightly feminine kind of way. A strange description, I know, but perhaps it was because he didn't have any hardness about him. Although I was hoping he was going to have plenty of hardness elsewhere.

'What were you thinking just then?' he asked.

I almost spat my wine everywhere, my eyes wide with embarrassment. 'Why do you ask?'

'The look on your face. You looked... naughty.' He almost sounded like Nicholas Cage, too! Especially the way he said 'naughty'. Ooh.

'Well then, I must have been thinking naughty thoughts,' I said sensuously. At least I hoped it was sensuous.

He stood up, and I couldn't help eyeing his crotch—yes, there was hope for hardness, alright. I became warm at the thought, and my face flushed a little.

'We should get going, I made the reservation for 8.15, and I think we'll be a bit late, but it shouldn't matter too much.'

'Where are we going?'

'That's a secret.'

He helped me into my coat. I picked up my handbag, found my keys, and we were off.

At 8.25 we arrived at a cosy little Italian restaurant in the suburbs. We were shown immediately to a romantic table in a secluded corner, where we ordered a bottle of red wine, tomatoes with mozzarella to start, followed by ravioli for Grayson and spaghetti carbonara for me. I'd ordered it before realising how messy spaghetti could be. Oops.

The food and wine were delicious, and the company perfect. This time Grayson wanted to know everything about me. And after a few more glasses, I even told him about Russell and my mother. He placed his hand over mine on the table and laughingly told me he'd steer clear of her in the future then, and perhaps he should have a description of her considering she lived close by.

I giggled, but inside my heart, fluttered.

The sound of his voice began to turn me on, and soon enough, he was gazing into my eyes and telling me that he'd love to see me again, and again, and again.

'I feel that we really click, Summer. You're a beautiful woman, with a great personality, and I feel that I can tell you anything. I'm hoping you feel the same way. I know this is only our first date—not counting McDonald's the other day, that is,' he laughed shyly, 'and if I'm moving too fast, I'll back off. Just say the words.'

Wow, what a speech. I hoped this wasn't going to be too good to be true. I pinched myself, just to make sure I wasn't dreaming. Luckily for me, I wasn't. I had a nice red pinch mark to prove it. This was real life, although it felt more like a daytime soap opera unfolding before my very eyes.

'Well, I don't want you to back off. I'd really love to see you again and again too. You're pretty hot stuff too, you know!' I replied with a smile, and he squeezed my hand. I gazed into his deep brown eyes, desire growing by the second.

He paid the bill, and we drove home in silence. I was thinking of the perfect way to invite him in without sounding tarty, tacky or desperate. He was probably wondering whether I was going to invite him in as well.

When he eventually pulled up outside the flat, we turned to each other. 'W-would y-you like to come in for a drink?'

There, I'd managed to say it, and it hadn't sounded too bad.

'I'd really like that.'

Inside, after taking off my boots (and secretly spraying my feet with perfume), I poured us some more wine and then went to put on some music. Barry White? Too obvious. Guns n Roses? Too loud. Madonna's Like a Virgin? I laughed—I don't think so. George Michael's I Want Your Sex? Er, definitely not! So, I settled for Ed Sheeran. Perhaps a bit soppy at times, but it'd do.

We both stood drinking, listening to music, wondering what was going to happen next. I decided to make the first move. I approached him, put both our glasses down and said, 'Would you like to dance?'

Talk about tacky.

'Sure.' He took me in his arms and held me close while we basically smooched along to Ed's Thinking Out Loud. I started to imagine the music video and wished he would whisk me off my feet. But it didn't take long for me to feel something rather large and rather hard pressing against me. I looked up, and he kissed me.

Boy, what a kiss. It made me feel like jelly in his arms. Before long I'd undone his shirt, taken it off and thrown it across the room. Mmmm, nice chest. Off came his shoes and socks (fortunately not Mickey Mouse) and then his trousers. Much to my delight, he was wearing boxers (I'm not a big fan of briefs and Y-fronts, urgh), which I let him keep on. For a little while, anyway. Then I pulled away from him and pushed him onto the sofa.

I'd obviously had a bit too much (perhaps an understatement) to drink, because I began to dance in front of him, slowly removing the dress and letting it drop to the floor. When it dawned on him that all I was wearing were hold-up stockings, he gasped with pleasure. He tried to get up, but I waved my finger at him as if he were a naughty schoolboy.

'No…sit and watch', I drawled, as I bent and caressed my thighs cheekily in front of him.

If I'd have suddenly become sober, I would have died from embarrassment, but I was so drunk I couldn't care less. In fact, I started to imagine I was Demi Moore in Striptease. Only I was naked and touching myself. But boy, was it having the most amazing effect on Grayson. He was so hard I thought he would explode. But I didn't stop. I turned my back to him and bent at the waist, fortunately, my yoga classes had paid off, as I was able to look at him from between my thighs, 'D'you think I'm hot?' I whispered.

He nodded, unable to speak.

I finally turned back around to face him, gently removed his shorts and sank down onto him. Wowweeee, I thought.

Finally, he managed to speak. 'So now I know why you were having naughty thoughts earlier,' he whispered, as he gently caressed the soft flesh of my boobs, bending down to take a nipple in his mouth. He sure had a great way of tantalisingly teasing it between his teeth.

I groaned. God that was so good.

It became a bit rougher. Not nastily rough, but wickedly and enthusiastically vigorous. Mmmmm. Wow. Yeah (baby yeah).

He touched me in all the right places, and he seemed to know exactly what I liked.

Eventually, we made it to the bedroom, after an hour or so in the living room and kitchen, where we'd had orgasm after orgasm after orgasm throughout the night.

And no…this time I wasn't dreaming, but boy did it feel like it.

This week had turned out to be one of the best weeks of my life. This guy made Russell look like a complete wet fart in bed. And Russell had actually been rather good!

CHAPTER 4

I was woken up by the curtains being opened, and a voice I didn't recognise at first. 'Rise and shine, sleepyhead.'

I opened my eyes, wondering what the hell was going on. It was Grayson, and he'd made breakfast and brought it to me in bed. My God, was there no end to this amazing guy?

'Hi, gorgeous, did you sleep well?' he asked.

'Well I didn't get a great deal of it, but neither did you, for that matter,' I giggled. 'I can't believe you made me breakfast in bed. Nobody has ever done this for me before. It's lovely. But you really didn't have to, you know.'

'I know that. But I wanted to. Last night, by the way, was amazing. The Earth moved.'

Oh, God, I remembered the striptease. How embarrassing. But hang on a minute, did he just say the Earth moved? Now that was tacky. Finally, there was something wrong with him, but then I realised he'd been joking. I smirked, and he started to laugh.

'I wanted to see your face if I said something like that.'

'Well, ha dee haha,' I said, munching away on a piece of toast and slurping over a cup of tea. I must have looked a right mess—I sure felt like a mess. Jesus…how much had I drank?

'The little striptease was absolutely fantastic, though. Actually… do you even remember that?'

Puce with embarrassment, I nearly coughed chewed up toast all over him as I nodded and cringed.

'Don't be embarrassed. You were amazing. Better than any strippers I've ever seen before.'

I smiled, hoping he hadn't really seen that many if any at all.

'So do you have any plans today?' he asked.

'Not really, do you?' I replied.

'Yes.'

I must have looked disappointed because he suddenly broke out in a big grin and said, 'My plans do involve you, though.'

'You're not some kind of mass murderer, are you? You're not planning on hacking me to pieces all day or something?' I asked, smirking, not knowing entirely where that had come from. Maybe I'd been watching too many movies, although lately, the majority of my pastimes consisted of watching Dirty Dancing, Legally Blonde and Twilight. Not exactly murderers galore. Well, not counting the vampires.

'Aw, shucks, you got me,' he said as he began to tickle me.

After another hour or so of more intoxicating sex under a hot shower, we got dressed and headed over to his place so he could change into some clean clothes.

While he was changing, I had a little snoop around his apartment. It was immaculate and tidy. Very well decorated. He had good taste. But it did seem to have a woman's touch to it, which was a bit odd. There were a few vases with fresh flowers in them, but the most curious thing was that he had several women's magazines... Cosmopolitan, Marie Claire... Good Housekeeping and stuff like that. I thought perhaps they'd belonged to his ex-girlfriend, but I was sure he'd told me they'd broken up about six months ago, and these magazines were current editions.

When he came out of his bedroom, he saw me leafing through them. His initial reaction was surprise, but then he said, 'You're probably thinking how strange it is for a guy to have all the latest women's magazines. Well, it's actually for work. I'm encouraged to check out the latest kind of photography and stories.'

'Not a bad idea, I suppose,' I muttered.

I'm sure I heard him breathe a sigh of relief. I guess I should have thought a bit more of it at the time, but I was so smitten with him that anything weird would have seemed totally reasonable.

'So what are we going to do now?' I asked.

'Today is your day, gorgeous. What would you like to do?'

'I thought you said you had plans?'

'My plans are spending the weekend with you and doing exactly what you want to do.'

'Now don't give me the responsibility of making a decision like that, I'm terrible at thinking of things to do, except for shopping, and I doubt that you want to do that.'

'Well, if that's what you really want to do, we could. Or…we could go to the zoo, go to the park, go ice-skating, go to the cinema, or we could rent out a few videos and have a very lazy day making love, consuming copious amounts of alcohol and stuffing ourselves silly with crisps, nuts, pizzas, ice cream, et cetera, et cetera.'

'Wow, you're full of ideas, aren't you? And you're serious about all of that stuff?'

'Completely and utterly serious,' he said with his arms on his hips like Peter Pan.

'Okay, let's rent some movies, go buy some booze, some food and more importantly…some condoms!' I chuckled.

He scooped me up over his shoulder and carried me outside to the car.

'Supermarket, here we come,' he whooped as I screamed with laughter.

We bought several bottles of wine and lager, a bottle of peach schnapps, lots and lots of crisps, a few pizzas, chocolates and ice-cream and a large box of condoms.

This was, without a doubt, my kinda guy!

This time I insisted he let me at least pay half the bill. He argued at first, but being my usual stubborn self, he finally conceded, bearing in my mind that, basically, he didn't have a choice.

So then we headed back to his place for a weekend of pure bliss. I could hardly wait.

We put on Netflix and decided in advance what movies we

would spend the day watching. I figured this would be a good way of getting to know him better, to see what kind of films he would pick, but unfortunately, he seemed to want whatever I chose, so we settled on some old ones: Gladiator, Notting Hill, Runaway Bride and The Sixth Sense.

'Julia Roberts looks so great in that dress. It certainly does her justice,' he muttered.

'Huh? Yeah, great,' funny thing for a bloke to say. He obviously just fancied the pants off her but didn't want to say so.

'And those shoes, aren't they super?' he began again, but quickly mumbled, 'Er, I mean, they'd look great on you. Maybe next week, we could go shopping for you.'

'Are you trying to tell me that you don't like my clothes?' I bickered.

'No, of course not. It's just that one of the things you said you liked doing is shopping, and I thought it would be nice to go with you.'

What? A man who likes clothes shopping. Get outta here.

'You enjoy clothes shopping?' I gasped, almost choking on a Monster Munch.

'Erm. Yes, actually. I'm your regular new millennium man. I want to do everything with you…even shopping. So do we have a date? Next weekend, at least one day of shopping?'

I was in shock. Was this guy for real? 'Y-y-yeah, sure. That'd be great. Is there a special occasion that I need a new outfit for?' I questioned.

'Well, I am supposed to be covering a fashion show by Esra Suopmop next week, and that's quite a formal event. I'd quite like you to join me'.

'The Esra Suopmop?!' I shrieked. He was the next best thing since Armani, and Grayson wanted me to join him. Hell yes, of course, I would go.

I threw my arms around him, knocking over a bowl of crisps at the same time. 'Oh, shit! Sorry, I'll get that,' I muttered, still smiling at the thought of me going to a fashion show of such a hotshot.

Grayson turned his attention back to the film as I cleaned up the mess.

'Where are your plastic bags?'

'In one of the drawers in the kitchen. I'll get one for you.'

'No, don't. I knocked them over, I'll sort them out. I'll get it,' I replied, jumping up and heading to the next room. Opening the drawers, I saw that one was full of make-up. I gasped. Why the hell did he have make-up in his kitchen drawer? I just stood there trying to figure it out, and I was still stood there looking at it when Grayson walked in.

'You're taking your time, aren't...' he came to a sudden halt as he stared at the drawer.

'Is there something you have to tell me, Grayson?' I whispered.

He was quite red in the face and seemed to be searching for the right thing to say. 'I can imagine exactly what you're thinking, Summer, and it is not what it looks like,' he mumbled. 'This stuff doesn't belong to me, and it doesn't belong to my ex, either.'

'Then who the hell does it belong to, Grayson? Are you some kind of freak? Are you seeing someone else? Tell me, are you two-timing me? Tell me!' I was so angry. I finally meet a really nice guy, and then this happens. I guess I had a bit of cheek, yelling. After all, we'd only been seeing each other a couple of days.

'Actually, love, you've got it all wrong,' he said, with quite an embarrassed smile. 'It belongs to my...er...younger... sister'.

Did I feel like a total fool, or did I feel like a total fool?

'Oh God, Grayson, I'm so sorry. I feel like such a prat, accusing you of being some kind of cross-dressing two-timing freak. I should have known better.'

I bowed my head in shame as he began to chuckle and came over to give me a hug.

'I would have thought exactly the same thing, Summer, it's okay. It is kind of funny, though, isn't it? I mean, can you really picture me wearing all this make-up and dressing up in women's clothes and going out for a wander downtown?'

I hadn't exactly accused him of doing any of those things, but I guess it was a funny thought, so I laughed too.

'So, you're probably still wondering why my sister's make-up is here. Well, she's only fourteen, and our parents don't let her wear make-up, but I do. So sometimes she comes round here to put it on before she goes out with friends.'

I listened and wondered why he hadn't mentioned her before, but then figured we'd only been seeing each other for a couple of days. I should give him time.

'So, what's her name?' I asked.

'Whose name?'

I gave him a funny look, and it dawned on him that I was referring to his sister.

'Oh, er, yea—my sister. Er... Emily, that's it. Her name that is.'

I thought he'd reacted a bit weirdly, but I suppose considering I'd just accused him of being a cross-dresser, it was okay. 'Do you have any photos of her?' I asked.

He said that he didn't and quickly changed the subject, as he finally closed the offending drawer and took out a plastic bag from another, which I took from him and went back to the lounge to clean up the mess from the floor.

'I think it's a good time for a drink,' he hollered from the kitchen, 'What would you like?'

'I'll have whatever you're having.'

He came back into the room with a couple of beers and some more nibbles, and we settled back in front of the telly to watch the rest of the movies.

CHAPTER 5

*G*rayson dropped me back at my flat on Sunday night, and we kissed passionately in his car before saying our good-nights. We'd agreed not to act like we were dating in front of everybody at work, to avoid any unpleasant and potentially embarrassing situations from some of the bozos that worked there. I need not mention names.

Following the bizarre occurrences of Saturday evening though, Grayson had not once mentioned Emily and the make-up, and she hadn't turned up at any point throughout the weekend which I thought was a bit odd, considering young girls usually like to go out with their friends on Saturdays and Sundays. Anyway, I'd decided not to mention anything, as it had seemed a bit of a sore point.

Gwen came downstairs as soon as I opened my front door. 'My, my...who is this stranger walking into Summer's flat?' she smiled. 'So, sweetie, you've obviously been enjoying yourself this weekend! Come on, I want to know all the gory details,' she chuckled.

'I'm absolutely knackered, Gwen. I've hardly slept all weekend,' I said with a wicked grin, 'and we drank so much. I could really use a lovely cup of coffee, or two. Do you fancy one?'

'Why don't you sit down and start talking, and I'll make it?' she offered, as we walked into the kitchen.

I did as I was told and began reeling off what had been going on during the last couple of days. '....and then he acted a bit weird, almost like he couldn't remember her name, which was Emily, by the way. He didn't have any pictures of her, and she didn't come around at all. I know it was pretty nasty of me to assume the worst, but it was a bit weird. It's not every day that you find make-up in your boyfriend's kitchen...'

'Did you inspect his bedroom and bathroom to see if he had anything else weird?' she interrupted.

'Why would I do that when he offered up a perfectly feasible explanation?'

'I don't buy it. The guy sounds weird, Summer.'

'How can you say that? Just because of that one thing? Give him a break, for God's sake.'

'Don't be so naïve. I mean, first you said he collects women's magazines, then he's got make-up, he wants to go clothes shopping with you, he claims to have a sister whose name he wasn't so sure about? Plus, he's obsessed with Julia Roberts' clothes. Need I say more?' she exclaimed.

Getting angry, I stormed into my bedroom to change and shouted, 'God, what is your problem? I finally meet a really great guy who really likes me and wants to have a relationship with me, and all you can do is start going on and on about him like he's some sort of weirdo. He's attractive, sexy, great in bed, and he likes me,' I walked back into the kitchen and poured another cup of coffee. 'So stop going on. Oh, hang on. I get it. You're jealous, aren't you?'

'Me? Jealous? Why the hell would I be jealous? That you've started dating some weird bloke who's got something to hide? I don't think so.'

'Well, I do,' I yelled back.

'You know what?' Gwen said. 'You're turning into your mother!' With that, she turned and stormed out.

That was, without doubt, the worst insult anyone could ever pay me. My mother wasn't exactly up there with my other idols: Madonna and Marilyn Monroe.

Who the hell did she think she was, anyway? Having a go like that. She was obviously jealous. Jealous of me dating such a great catch like Grayson. Well, she can just get stuffed, I thought, as I began running a nice hot bubble bath.

While I lay there soaking, I thought about what Gwen had said. I didn't want to think about it, but I just couldn't help it. But I soon came to the conclusion that Grayson was perfectly normal. After all, everybody had a certain amount of skeletons in their closet, and I was pretty sure that his skeletons weren't any worse than the average Joe's. Gwen was just paranoid. I decided to give her a couple of days to calm down, and then I'd go and make up.

I was so exhausted that I nodded off and nearly bloody drowned. I woke with a start as I swallowed some bathwater. I coughed and spluttered and got water all over the bathroom floor, so I jumped out before I did some serious damage. Soon afterwards, I was curled up in bed asleep like a heavily-medicated baby.

The next couple of days went pretty smoothly. I hardly saw Grayson, as he had lots of stories to cover, although he did call on Monday night, just to say hi and make sure I was feeling okay after all the alcohol we'd consumed over the weekend. He told me he couldn't see me until Saturday morning because he had stuff to do every night, but he arranged to pick me up at nine to start the shopping spree.

'Make sure you get plenty of rest until then. You'll need it. I probably won't see you in the office either, because I'm doing a bit of extra work for the other newspapers this week. Take care, babe. I'll see you on Saturday.'

I must admit, I hadn't really been too bothered; I looked forward to having some more me-time.

On Tuesday evening, I popped up to see Gwen to apologise for being a bit of a bitch, but she wasn't there. She must have been out with Hugh, so instead, I decided to go and see my mum. After all, I hadn't seen her for at least a month.

'Hello? Who is it?' fluttered the voice on the other side of the door.

'Mum, it's me. Summer,' I answered, wishing she would stop trying to sound so sexy

She opened the door, stepped quickly outside and pulled the door closed behind her. 'Honeybun, sweetie! How are you? What a lovely surprise. A little unexpected, though,' she whispered as she gave me a hug and two air kisses.

'Hi, Mum. I'm fine,' I said, trying to get past her into her little apartment. She seemed to pull me back and was obviously delaying our entry. I figured she must have another bloke in there.

'So who is it this time, Mum?'

She reddened a little and put her head down. 'No-one you know, sweetheart.'

Which meant it was someone I knew.

I pushed past her and opened the door, only to be greeted by one of the most unpleasant and horrendous sights of my entire life. All twenty-four years of it.

My boss, Jack Willoughby, was crouched over—bollock naked —on all fours on top of the coffee table. He was utterly oblivious to the fact that my mother had opened the front door, and he looked as though he was waiting to be spanked. Suddenly, in a John Wayne-type accent, he yelled out, 'Ooh, spank me, darlin', spank me,' but as he turned, he finally realised that he and my lovely mother were not alone. He unceremoniously fell off the table and grabbed a cushion to hide his credentials; incidentally, a matchstick would probably have done the job.

I gasped and heaved, feeling totally nauseous all of a sudden. This was not a pretty sight. I quickly shot out of the front door.

My mother followed me. 'Summer, wait, honey. Sweetie!'

'Did you know he was my boss, Mum?' I asked.

She said nothing

'Well... Did you?'

'He told me where he worked, so I figured it out myself. But he doesn't know you're my daughter. Well, at least he didn't know, anyway. But please, pumpkin, don't tell your colleagues about this. I rather like him, and I wouldn't want this little scene to stop him from seeing me again,' she said as she battered her eyelids.

Realising that my silly blonde bimbo of a mother and Mr Nega-tivity were probably very well matched, I told her I wouldn't tell all my colleagues (the all was lost on her).

As she lived reasonably close to Grayson, I decided to walk round to see if he was home. As I walked, the hilarity of the situation suddenly hit me, and I smiled, then I began to laugh, and laugh and laugh and laugh and laugh and laugh. The people walking down the street beside me gave me the oddest looks, but some of them began to laugh, too; it was almost like it was contagious. It was really rather amusing.

As I approached Grayson's street, I noticed a tall woman with long blond hair coming out of his flat. She was wearing a bright pink tight dress with extremely high pink stilettos, which she had great difficulty walking in. The bastard. So, he was seeing someone else. She was wearing an awful lot of make-up...oh! Maybe it was Emily. Ah-ha, so now I had the chance to meet her. As I walked past his flat, I noticed there were no lights on, so he must have been out... unless he was in bed.

The woman was quite a distance away, but I yelled after her anyway.

'Emily! Emily!' but she didn't turn around. That's a bit on the weird side, I thought, she does seem a bit tall and tarty for a fourteen-year-old. I decided to follow her and find out who she really was.

I soon realised she was headed towards the local red-light district. Oh God, she's a hooker. Grayson has been seeing a hooker. I couldn't believe it. For the second time that night, I felt very nauseous, but I carried on following her. Finally, she stopped on a street corner, opened her handbag, took out a lipstick and carefully applied another coat. She flicked her hair this way and that and then pushed up her boobs and squeezed them together. Finally, she hitched up her dress, revealing stockings and suspenders beneath it. God, what a tart.

Not surprisingly, it didn't take long for her to be picked up by a weird-looking couple in a Mercedes.

Utterly miserable at the thought of my wonderful boyfriend having sex with a hooker, I slowly walked home, tears stinging my eyes and the cold making my nose and ears feel like icicles. I contemplated waiting outside Grayson's until he got back but came to the conclusion that there was no point. I felt like an absolute idiot. I'd even fallen out with my best pal in the whole world over this prick. The one person that was right about him in the first place. Gwen. My best friend. I really needed her.

Fortunately, she was home by the time I got there, so I knocked on the door, feeling like a total, helpless wreck.

'Who is it?' she yelled.

'It's me, Gwen.'

'What do you want?' she asked as she opened the door, looking angrier than ever, but her face softened the minute she laid eyes on me.

'Oh God, Summer, what's happened? You look terrible.' She took my hands. 'Jeeze, girl, yer freezin.' She helped me take off my coat and sat me down in the lounge next to the radiator. 'I'll be right back,' she said as she walked into the kitchen.

Five minutes later she returned with coffee and brandy for us both. Then she sat down next to me. 'Now tell me. What on Earth has happened?'

I began to cry again, and soon I was howling so much that I had great difficulty in getting the words out, 'Longest night of my life... Mum...Negativity...spanking... Grayson...Emily... Hooker...fucking...hooker... Hooker...fuck, fuck, fuck,' I sobbed and sobbed as Gwen handed me tissue after tissue after tissue.

'Oh, you poor thing. Your mum is sleeping with your boss? Is that right?'

I nodded.

'And Grayson is sleeping with a hooker?'

I nodded again.

'Are you sure?'

Again, I nodded.

I eventually calmed down a bit and was able to explain what had happened and what I'd seen.

She found the Jack and my mum business positively hilarious, but only laughed when I'd completely finished crying.

She was such a good friend. I apologised for the Sunday night incident and for doubting what she said. She'd obviously been entirely right about Grayson, I just wished I hadn't been so naïve.

'That's alright, Summer. I'm sorry too—especially for saying that thing about you and your mum. I really didn't mean it. You're really nothing like your mum. I mean, you'd never sleep with ol' Negativity!' she laughed.

Despite myself, I laughed too, and together we pictured the scene again, Jack on the coffee table singing 'spank me darlin', spank me'.

Gwen cheered me up no doubt, and I told her that I never wanted to see that creep Grayson ever again. I mean, if he was sleeping with a hooker, he could have some sexually transmitted disease, which meant he could have passed it on to me. Urgh, just the thought made me itch.

We decided I would take the following day off work. Jack certainly wasn't going to complain, under the circumstances, and Gwen didn't work anyway, so a day looking after me was great, as far as she was concerned.

I stayed at Gwen's place that night; I didn't want to be alone. I couldn't handle it. So we stayed up most of the night watching all her great DVDs, especially all the ones with hunks in them, to try and make me feel better, such as Dirty Dancing (yes, again), Ghost, Cocktail (although the part where he goes off with the older tart didn't really help), The Matrix (maybe what happened to me didn't really happen because it wasn't really the 'real' world?), Lethal Weapon (Mel Gibson's bum always makes me feel better), as well as the usual original Footloose (Kevin Bacon's moves were always helpful too). We ate quite a large amount of ice-cream and had, finally, fallen asleep on the sofa at about six in the morning.

I woke up at midday, feeling very much at peace with myself. I'd come to realise that it wasn't such a big thing losing Grayson, considering we hadn't really been dating that long, but my main concern was the whole sex disease thing. We'd decided that I should go and get checked out at the doctors. Gwen said she'd go with me for support. I hated going to see the doctor, so getting checked out 'down there' was a fate almost worse than death.

Fortunately, Grayson wasn't around during the week, so he could easily be avoided. I hadn't quite decided what I was going to do or say to him, and I really didn't want to see him anyway. I didn't want anything to do with him. He'd turned out to be one major arsehole.

On the way to the clinic, I seemed to develop a real itch in the groin area, and I was pretty sure it was mainly due to paranoia, but still, I had to be sure.

'Are you alright?' asked Gwen as I kept discreetly scratching myself. At least, I hope it was discreet.

'Yeah, I'll be fine, I guess I'm just a bit paranoid about this whole thing. Don't worry about me, I'll get over it.' I smiled, although inside I felt like a corpse.

We waited for about an hour to be seen at the clinic before I was asked to pee in a plastic cup. I was in the loo for quite a while trying to squeeze a drop out. Finally, I managed it and was quite proud of myself. The nurse who I handed it to, however, looked at it in disappointment. And then finally I heard the receptionist screech, 'Miss Miller, the doctor will see you now. The second door on your left.' 'I'll be right here, Luv. Don't worry, you'll be alright,' comforted Gwen.

I walked into the doctor's room and came face to face with one of the most gorgeous men I'd ever laid eyes on. God, did I want to run?

'Good morning, Miss Miller, please take a seat. I'm Dr Short,' he said as he stood, all six foot five of him, and shook my hand.

'G-g g-g-good morning, Dr Short.'

That's a name which couldn't be further from the truth, I thought, as I looked the tall, handsome, well-built doctor up and down.

'So, let's get right down to it, shall we? First, have you suffered from any sexually transmitted diseases before?' Now I understood why the receptionist had already asked me what I thought was wrong.

I turned crimson. 'No, never,' I answered.

'And what makes you think you may have contracted one?'

'Er, well, I... I...' Oh, God, it was so embarrassing. 'I had sexual intercourse with someone who may have had intercourse with a..a...prostitute.' There, I'd managed to spit it out.

He nodded. 'Have you had peculiar itching or burning sensations?'

'Not really. Basically, I just wanted to rule it out,' I replied.

He smiled and said, 'That's very wise, Miss Miller. Now, we should have a look to see if there is anything to worry about. Please take off your trousers and underwear and put on this smock. Then, I'll be right back,' he said, as he quietly exited another door. I carefully took off my clothes and put on the funny white shirt thingy, which showed my white bum from behind.

A couple of minutes later, he was back.

I stood like a complete moron awaiting instructions.

'Okay, Miss Miller, please sit up here and place your legs in these stirrups. That's it. Nurse, we're ready for you now,' a nurse came into the room and stood behind me, just to make sure no funny business went on.

I was so nervous about this hunk-of-a-doctor that he said, 'Please try and relax, Miss Miller, this won't hurt a bit. Relax. That's it. Good.'

The problem was he was so gorgeous I could feel myself actually getting a little bit hot. Think horrible thoughts, think horrible thoughts. Think false teeth, dog poo, heart transplants, war, spring onions, tripe, George Bush and sick and hangovers. Horrible thoughts. Horrible thoughts. Horrible thoughts. It obviously worked because before I knew it, he'd finished. Thank God.

'Okay, if you'd like to get down and get dressed now, please, and then come and sit here by my desk.'

After I was dressed, he explained that everything seemed to be fine, but there were a couple of tests which still had to be done. He took a blood sample, and of course, he already had the urine sample, so he said I would be telephoned in a few days with the results.

I smiled and shook his hand, thanking him for seeing me.

Gwen stood up the second she saw me and whispered, 'So, is everything okay?'

'Yep, so far so good, but they still have to do some tests. They'll call me with the results in a couple of days.'

'But were you okay in there, with the doctor and the internal thingy? I know how awful they can be…'

'Oh, that—no, it went fine. In fact, it went better than fine. You should see the doctor. What a man…' I drawled.

'You tart,' she whispered.

As it was quite a sunny day for a change, we decided to get some air and walk home.

'So, what am I going to do about Grayson?' I asked as we stopped to peer into a shop window, only to realise it was one of those hardcore sex shops, so we hurried on, a bit pink in the face.

'Well, I've been giving it some thought, and I wondered about having a little dinner party. We could track down the hooker and invite her—or rather, we could pay her to join us. Can you imagine Grayson's face? It'd be a right picture. It'd definitely be worth shelling out fifty quid or so. What do you reckon?' she said, nudging my arm.

I wasn't too sure about it. It was cruel, but he was cruel, too, leading me on like that. 'But, but how would we find the hooker?'

'That's easy enough, Summer. You said you followed her to where she got picked up. It's more than likely that'll be her spot. If we went back there one night, she'd probably be doing her stuff. We'd have to get there pretty early to talk to her, of course, before she's picked up.'

'I don't know, Gwen. The last thing I want to be seen doing is talking to a prostitute. Couldn't we get someone else to do it?'

She put her arm in mine, and we continued walking. 'Sweetie, it'd be a right blast. Live a little, why don't you? First, all we have to do is talk to her. I think it's a grand idea. Where's yer sense of adventure?' she giggled. 'Besides, he deserves it.'

Reluctantly I agreed, and we decided to try and find her the following night.

'That's the spirit. But what are you going to say to Grayson in the meantime? If you completely diss him, he's gonna know something's up. You're gonna have to pretend you don't know owt.'

'Well, that shouldn't be too difficult. Apparently, he's pretty busy at the moment. Plus, we agreed not to act like a couple at work so, even if I completely ignored him, he'd just go with it and not suspect a thing.'

The two of us spent the rest of the day just hanging around my flat, talking and watching talk shows on TV. One of them was about men who were revealing to their partners that they were in fact, cross-dressers, and when they were alone at home, they'd get dressed up in their partner's clothes (underwear and all) and make-up. Halfway through the show, they were taken backstage and then at the very end, came back in all dressed up as women. One woman even fainted. It was quite shocking, actually.

'No way,' we shouted.

'Oh, my God! Can you imagine? If that ever happened to me, I'd die. I'd die. Especially on national TV. Do these people have no shame?' I exclaimed.

'Absolutely not. They can't have. Sometimes I think these shows are all made up. Some of the people must be actors. I mean, they must be,' Gwen said. 'Anyway, I'm going to put the kettle on. Do you fancy a cuppa?'

I nodded and turned my attention back to the TV. One poor woman was explaining that when she'd first started dating her boyfriend, she'd suspected something a bit odd. She kept finding make-up at his house, he loved clothes shopping with her, and he seemed to be obsessed with women's magazines, but she'd ignored the signs because she'd been totally head over heels for him.

Suddenly it dawned on me, and I felt like the world's biggest fool.

'Gwen… Gwen! Come here, quick!' I yelled, shaking all over.

'What is it?' she said as she rushed in. I pointed to the TV and Gwen listened to the woman.

'I've just realised something, and I feel like an absolute pillock. How could I have been so naïve and stupid? Oh God!' I leaned forward and put my head in my hands. 'I've just put two and two together. Grayson. Do you remember I said that the woman who left his house looked like him? I assumed it had been his sister, but then realised she was a bit too old. It was him. It had to be. That's why he had make-up in his kitchen. My initial reaction was right.' I shook my head in disbelief. 'I've been dating—and worse still, I've been having sex with—a cross-dressing male prostitute,' I blurted out as I stood up, my whole body shaking.

Gwen was trying so hard not to laugh, I could see it in her eyes.

'Oh, for God's sake just do it, will you? Go ahead…laugh, I know you want to.'

But she managed to stifle it a bit longer. 'Look, I know this is totally and utterly unbelievable. I understand that. How anybody could do that to anyone else is beyond me. It's absolutely disgusting. But at least you've been to see a doctor, and you've pretty much been given the all-clear. I realise that it's far too soon to see the funny side and I'm sorry, b-b-but—' Then the laughter came.

She constantly giggled for about an hour, practically rolling about on the floor. She even locked herself in the bathroom and tried to think of sad things. But nothing worked. My best friend was finding my misery and tragedy highly amusing.

Finally, eyes red and sore and cheeks aching, she stopped.

'Oh, Summer. I'm so sorry. It's not you. It's the…it's the… he-whore!' she laughed again. But this time, I couldn't help it. I laughed too.

'Grayson The He-Whore,' we cried together.

'But what if I'm wrong, Gwen? What if he is normal and this hooker bore an uncanny resemblance to him?' I stopped temporarily to give him the benefit of the doubt.

'No way. You said yourself he buys women's magazines, has make-up in his kitchen drawer, came up with some excuse about a sister whose name he wasn't entirely sure about, wants to take you clothes shopping and, when you watched movies, all he went on about was what Julia Roberts was wearing. And on top of all that, you saw someone with a tremendous amount of make-up on, long blonde hair—which was probably a wig—a tarty little dress and high heels which she—he—it could hardly walk in, leave his apartment. Oh, and not to mention his comment at McDonald's about stockings and suspenders—I'll bet he was wearing them himself! And, of course, the TV show we just saw. Now, tell me. Do you still think he's a normal guy?'

I looked down and slowly shook my head

'I didn't think so,' she said.

CHAPTER 6

The next day I decided to go to work. Thankfully, Grayson wasn't there. Unfortunately, Mr Negativity was.

'Good morning, Summer!' he said as he walked past my desk. I was so taken aback that I nearly fell off my swivel chair.

'Shit,' I muttered in shock as I regained my balance. 'Morning, Jack.'

Suddenly I couldn't help but picture him at my mum's flat, naked on all fours on the coffee table begging to be spanked. I sniggered. It was apparent he noticed, and he quickly rushed outside for a cigarette.

I came to the conclusion that he was either going to be a complete arsehole or he was going to become Mr Positivity. Either way, I really couldn't give a shit, considering the recent discovery regarding my 'bitch' of a boyfriend.

Life certainly was a bitch at that moment, and unfortunately, I just had to live it—at the Gazette of all places.

After my snigger, Jack was neither pleasant nor unpleasant. He simply acted as if I wasn't there, which was fine by me. Unfortunately, it seemed to create a sense of mystery among some of the other members of staff. Jack was usually bitching about me—or at me—and they couldn't work out what had caused this change in attitude.

I contemplated standing on my desk and making an announcement, 'Hear Ye, Hear Ye! 3 o'clock and all is not well! Jack Willoughby gets off on getting bollock naked, crouching like a dog on tables and begging to be spanked, particularly by my mother. Hear Ye, Hear Ye!'

The thought brought me quite a great deal of pleasure, but no matter how much of a bitch I wanted to be, I just couldn't. Besides, even though she deserved it, I couldn't do that to my mother.

And while I was thinking of making announcements, I supposed I could also climb on to my desk—no, not my desk, the middle of Trafalgar Square would be more appropriate, with rather a large megaphone—and announce 'Hear Ye, Hear Ye, Grayson Rosenblum, photographer and reporter for The Monthly Gazette at The News Corporation, is, in fact, a He-Whore. A cross-dressing male hooking son-of-a-bitch who doesn't give a shit for anyone but himself! Hear Ye, Hear Ye!'

'Is everything alright, Summer?'

I practically jumped out of my skin, 'Wh…eh…what? Huh? Sorry?'

It was Jim. 'Are you alright? You looked really pissed off just then, almost as if you were going to stand up and murder some-one,' he said, concerned.

'Oh, yeah. I'm fine. I was in my own little world. Sorry, were you actually wanting me for something?'

'I was just making sure that you knew about the editorial meeting tomorrow afternoon, that's all.'

'Yes, but I'd forgotten all about it. Thanks for reminding me, Jim, I really appreciate it.'

'That's okay. It's just that you don't seem your usual self at the moment.' He began to walk away and then came back. 'Summer, are you sure you're okay? Did something bad happen? Is that why you were off yesterday? You look like you need a holiday or some-thing. Why don't you think about it, you could announce it at the meeting tomorrow,' he said, smiling.

He was so sweet, really.

'You know, that's a bloody good idea. Thanks for mentioning it.

It's nice to have a friend here,' I said sadly, purposefully omitting the distressing bits of my depressing and sad life lately.

That night I gave some serious thought to Jim's idea of taking a couple of weeks off. After the last few days, I could really use a break, so I decided to take a proper holiday. Luckily enough, I'd been saving my pennies for a break in the sun. I'd find out from Jack when I could go, and I'd have two whole weeks of sun, sea and fun. Hopefully, I could convince Gwen to join me. Considering that she didn't need to work because of her inheritance (sadly her parents had died in a car crash years earlier), she'd be able to afford it. I popped up to her flat there and then.

Convincing her was easy. All I did was mention the word holiday, and she replied, 'Wherever you go, sweetie, I'm there.'

So that was that. All we had to do was tell Jack, decide where to go, book it and wait patiently for the time to pass by.

oOo

THE FOLLOWING DAY WAS FRIDAY, and at the editorial meeting (Grayson wasn't there, he didn't really need to be) I told everyone that I needed a holiday and wanted to go as soon as possible.

Much to everyone's amazement, Jack suggested that I begin my vacation from that very weekend. 'We can cope for a couple of weeks without you, Summer. You go and enjoy yourself. In fact, why don't you try and grab a flight this weekend? You could get a good cheap deal taking a last-minute booking,' he'd said with the fakest of smiles.

If only the others had known why he was so happy for me to go! I decided to take him up on the offer and even left a bit early so I could book the trip.

After picking up loads of brochures from the local travel agent, I got home and checked the answerphone. I had two messages.

'Hello, Miss Miller, I'm calling from the clinic just to let you know that your test results are back. Would you please call back as soon as possible. Thank you. Goodbye,' said a shrill voice.

My initial reaction was, 'shit, they're bad, they must be otherwise she'd have said so on the phone'. I called back immediately.

'Hello. This is Miss Miller, calling for my test results.'

'One moment, please.'

I was put on hold for two long minutes, and to make matters worse the music was unbearable, similar to that tune, 'I know a song that'll get on your nerves, get on your nerves, get on your nerves, I know a song that'll get on your nerves, get on your nerves...'

'Miss Summer Miller?' said a smooth male voice on the other end of the line.

'That's me. Do you have my results?' I asked impatiently.

'Yes. They're all negative, Miss Miller. You're fine.'

Whooopdedooooo! 'Yes!' I shrieked.

The voice at the other end of the phone chuckled slightly. I thanked him and put it down, then I listened to the other message.

'Hi, gorgeous. It's Grayson. How are you doing? Okay, I hope. I just wanted a chat, that's all. Give me a call? Speak to you later. Bye.'

I sat down. He had such a lovely voice and had been so sexy. I put my head down onto the breakfast bar and sobbed. Why did this shit always have to happen to me?

I tried to pull myself together, thinking of my holiday and went upstairs to Gwen's flat. But before I got the chance to knock, I heard people's voices.

It was Gwen and Hugh, and they were having what sounded like quite a heated argument. Heated for them, anyway. Just a chat by anybody else's standards.

'Why didn't you tell me you were going on holiday? We could have gone together? Aw, come on, Gwen, we're supposed to be a couple, for God's sake.'

'Hugh, Summer is my best friend. She needs me right now. She's been having a few problems, and I need to help her sort them out. Just gi' me a break will you. You're always hassling me, and I don't need that right now. I need some time to think things through as well.'

'What is that supposed to mean? Don't you... Don't you want us to be together anymore?' he asked.

I leaned against the door, earwigging.

'That's not what I'm saying. I don't know, Hugh. Please, just give us a few weeks' break from each other. It'll do us a world of good. I'll give you my decision when we get back, okay?'

'But Gwen, I love you. I want you to be my wife. Please don't do this. Don't leave me,' he was almost sobbing, I could hear it in his voice.

'I know. All I'm asking is for a bit of time. No pressure from you. I need to do this, Hugh. Please understand.'

I could almost see him nod.

'So when are you planning on leaving?'

'I'm not sure yet. Whenever Summer can get the time off work.'

I figured this was my cue to knock.

The door opened, and in I pounced, pretending not to have heard a word of what was said. 'Good news, Gwen. We can leave this weekend! Oh, sorry, I hadn't realised Hugh was here. Hi, Huge Johnson! How's it hanging?'

Despite his evident heartbreak, Hugh liked me, and he grinned at my (by now) old joke. 'I'm fine, thanks. I hear you're going away for a couple of weeks. You take care of Gwen for me, okay?' he said as he gave her a peck on the cheek, and I nodded. 'Call me as soon as you get back, okay?' he said as he stroked Gwen's cheek with pain in his eyes. After saying goodbye, he left.

Gwen looked at me with tears in her eyes too. I gave her a hug. She knew I'd heard.

'Now the tables are turned, aren't they?' I said with a gentle smile.

After a couple of hours, a few glasses of wine and a bite to eat, we'd finally decided where to go on holiday. 'Algarve, here we come!' we said in unison as we clinked glasses, just moments after clicking on the 'Book' button online. I left Gwen to pack and went downstairs to get my own suitcase in order.

Grayson had phoned again and left a couple of messages. I wiped them off the machine. I didn't want to hear. He could turn up at my flat the next day to go shopping, and I simply wouldn't be there. That was his problem. I didn't give a shit. I was looking forward to my holiday too much for him to spoil it.

CHAPTER 7

*G*wen and I were all packed and ready to go at 05h00 the following morning. We sat and waited for the taxi to come and pick us up.

'So, what did you tell the He-Whore then?'

'Actually, I didn't tell him anything. As far as he's concerned, he's coming to pick me up at nine this morning to go on our shopping spree,' I said proudly.

Gwen chuckled at the thought. 'Good thinking Batman. By which time we shall be on a plane headed for the sunny Algarve. Great!'

Soon, the taxi arrived, and we sped off for the airport. There was one thing I was a bit peeved at though...the Esra Suopmop fashion show. Obviously, I wouldn't be going now. Oh well. A holiday was distinctly better...wasn't it?

We were so excited when we got on the plane. Nothing could possibly ruin our moods. We pushed all our problems to the backs of our minds and decided this holiday was going to be for us. No Hughs, no Graysons, no he-whores, no spanking, no negativity, no mothers. Just Gwen, me, sun, sand, sea and sangria—lots of it.

Neither of us had ever been to Portugal before, but we'd been told that the Algarve was a beautiful place. Perfect for sightseeing, catching the rays, swimming in the sea and great nightlife, and we'd been told that June was the ideal month to go. It was so exciting.

We chatted non-stop from the moment the plane took off until it landed, about two and a half hours later. Fortunately, the person who sat beside us was a perfectly normal Portuguese business-woman who didn't want any chitchat. Fine by us.

The second the seatbelt sign had blinked off, we jumped up and peered out of the window at Faro Airport.

'Well, it sure looks hot out there,' said Gwen as she removed her holdall from the overhead locker.

'It certainly does. I don't think I'll be needing this sweater,' I said as I took it off, revealing a tight pink T-shirt beneath it with my jeans and Converse.

Finally, we were slowly heading out of the plane, and as we reached the door and stepped outside, the force of the sun hit us. Pure bliss. It was so hot you could even see the heat haze sizzling off the runway.

After an hour or so waiting for our luggage, we finally sat on the coach and waited for it to take us to our hotel in Praia da Rocha. It was full of excited people, all pointing to the sights outside and to some of the dangerous driving we could see ahead of us. We'd heard on the plane that Portugal wasn't exactly known for its safety records and impeccable roads, but we managed to get to the hotel safely, and by the time we got there, there were only about ten people left on the coach. All of the others had been dropped off at hotels throughout the Algarve—Quarteira (what appeared to be a bit of a concrete jungle), Albufeira, and a sweet little tourist town called Praia do Carvoeiro had been just a few of the stops we'd made. A charming young couple named Sandra and David who were honeymooners and two other girls in their early twenties, Lisa and Amy, were staying at the same place as us.

Once we'd checked in and inspected our cosy little room, we donned our bikinis and headed straight down to the pool, where we stayed until seven that evening, turning regularly and rubbing in plenty of sun cream. Gwen was lucky, she wasn't as fair-skinned as me so she could get away with factor twenty, whereas I had to use factor fifty. Otherwise, I'd burn, blister, peel and go white again. Lucky me. I'd probably have to use fifty for the whole two weeks.

We stopped sunbathing briefly to grab a snack at the bar, where we'd met up, once again, with Lisa and Amy. They'd spent a couple of hours on the beach, checking out the local talent. They were clearly dying for it and asked if we wanted to go man hunting with them, but Gwen and I had decided we weren't interested in men at all this holiday. The whole idea was to get away from the men back home, so the last thing we wanted to do was get involved over here. But we did agree that a bit of harmless flirting was undoubtedly allowed, but told them we'd be a hindrance on their search, so they left without us.

That evening we donned a couple of cool little summer dresses and headed out to find a decent place to eat. We found a nice Portuguese restaurant with a friendly waiter who recommended a few dishes. We were willing to give anything a go, so we chose a table outside and sat back with a jug of sangria, a small bowl of black olives and waited for our starters to arrive.

After polishing off a plate of delicious yet tiny sardines, we noticed the waiter carrying a flaming plate, the flames reaching quite high.

'God, I wonder who's having that. Everyone's watching him. Look! I'd be so embarrassed if it were me,' chuckled Gwen, oblivious to the fact that he seemed to be heading straight in our direction.

Sure enough, he headed over and placed the sizzling, still-flaming plate down right in front of her. By the look on her face, she wanted to be gobbled up by the floor.

'Mmmm, that looks delicious. What is it?' I asked.

'Er, hang on a minute,' she said as she waited for the flames to die down, and pushed the food around her plate before realising what it was. 'Mmmmm, prawns. Here, try it,' she placed one on her fork and fed it to me. It was absolutely delicious.

Then my main course arrived: a plate full of squid. Not exactly my favourite, but once I'd tasted it, I soon changed my mind; the taste was out of this world. Gwen took a piece and nearly spat it out all over me.

I laughed. 'I guess you didn't like it, then?'

She screwed up her face in disgust. 'What's it called in Portuguese? I'll make sure not to order it in the next couple of weeks!'

'Erm, I can't remember. Hang on, I'll ask the waiter... Excuse me,' I said, waving in the air, and eventually, the elderly waiter saw me and headed straight over.

'Sím, yes?'

'Could you tell me what this is called in Portuguese, please?' I smiled sweetly.

'Is very good, yes? Is Lulas. Squid, yes? You like?' he stuttered.

'It's delicious. Very tasty, thank you.'

He bowed and returned inside the restaurant.

I wondered how Grayson had enjoyed his little shopping trip without me, and mentioned it to Gwen.

She laughed at the mere thought. 'Now you, I thought we'd agreed not to talk about him or any other of the bleedin' annoying blokes back home, this holiday?'

'Yeah, I know, but it's a bit difficult, isn't it? I mean, it must be tough for you. I know you don't want me to talk about it, but you don't want to leave Hugh, do you? I can see that you're in love with the guy.'

'I know. I am. But I haven't told him. Besides, I needed a break away from him, and I needed to see how he'd handle situations like these,' she said as she refilled our glasses with the sweet sangria.

'I must say, he sure did handle it well, didn't he? You're so lucky to have him. I wish I could find a nice bloke like him. You know, someone to treat me like a lady and to be there for me...'

'You mean someone like Grayson, who isn't a He-Whore?' she laughed.

'Well, I guess so. But even if it turned out that we'd really jumped to the wrong conclusions, why the hell did he have a hooker leaving his house?' I said, scrunching my eyebrows together.

'You really liked him, didn't you?'

'He's handsome, we have the same likes and dislikes, and he treated me very well when we were together—although it was only a few days. And he was amazing in bed. But he's turned out to be a major arsehole.'

As tears filled my eyes, Gwen handed me a tissue from her handbag and told me to try and forget him. After all, we'd come on holiday to forget about all those pricks back home. We were supposed to be having a good time.

So, after dinner, we took a walk down the strip to see what Praia da Rocha's nightlife was all about. It was heaving with people; locals and tourists alike. There were loads of street sellers, peddling paintings, ornaments, hair attachments, henna tattoos, jewellery and more. The atmosphere was fantastic.

Bar after bar stretched up the main street, and there were a fair amount of discos too, but we only had a couple of drinks in a small bar near the hotel and then went up to bed. After all, we had been up since four that morning and were exhausted. Plus, we intended to be bright and fresh for the following morning.

oOo

THE NEXT DAY we practically sprinted down to the beach. The sand was soft and warm, and there was a slight breeze, but the sea was absolutely bloody freezing. It didn't stop us from dipping in and out all day long though, to bring down our core temperatures, which were soaring. It was absolute heaven.

At midday, we went to a beach bar and ordered a couple of chicken salads and a bottle of vinho verde—green wine— called Gazela, which was cold, quite sweet and utterly delicious.

While we sat and talked, a couple of very attractive young men walked up the stairs and sat down at the table next to us. They clearly found us interesting and kept turning to have a look and a smile. Eventually, they began to chat with us and offered to buy us another bottle of wine. We took them up on their offer, and they moved from their table to ours. Wow, weren't we the lucky ladies? Lisa and Amy would be so jealous to see us with these two hunks.

They were Americans, who had just arrived, and were staying in Praia da Rocha for a couple of weeks, too. Both were tall and lean and very well built. One was fair-haired, with chiselled features and the most perfect bright white teeth; in fact, he looked like he should be in some kind of toothpaste commercial. His name was Brad, and he seemed a bit too perfect—for my taste, anyway. Not that it really mattered, as he appeared to be quite taken with Gwen. They told us they were staying at a hotel near ours.

The other was dark-skinned with shoulder-length shaggy black hair. He had the most beautiful deep brown eyes, but the thing that I really noticed about him was his hands. They were strong and very masculine yet very clean. I'd always thought it was essential for a man to have sexy hands (and a nice firm bum à la Mel Gibson, of course). His name was Ryan.

After lunch, they joined us down on the beach for the rest of the afternoon. Brad and Gwen spent the entire time chatting, although she made it quite clear that she was involved with someone and wasn't interested in having a holiday fling. Brad was clearly respectful of that and even confided that he was actually engaged to be married. This holiday was one last bit of fun with his best mate before he tied the knot in the autumn.

Following my recent escapades with the He-Whore, and my relationships with Russell and Aaron, I was beginning to feel that I deserved a bit of harmless fun. And as Ryan hadn't mentioned any women in his life, I made a point of making it clear that I was very much S.I.N.G.L.E. We were obviously very attracted to each other, anyway.

'How d'ya fancy a dip, Summer?' he drawled in his sexy southern accent.

I jumped up to join him, but he grabbed me and threw me over his shoulder as he ran down to the water's edge. He didn't have the slightest bit of trouble carrying me, which was pretty impressive; I didn't exactly consider my body weight to be particularly low.

I screamed and laughed. 'Put me down! Put me down! Noooo!' But it was too late. Seconds later, there was a loud splash as he carefully let me fall into the freezing water.

He grabbed me and pulled me up. The only problem was that I seemed to have lost my bikini top. But I hadn't even noticed, as it was so cold. I'm glad that he said something though because I'd been holding my stomach in, trying to stand upright, pushing my boobs out a bit—my feeble attempts to look sexy. And there I was, literally pushing my boobs out – erect nipples and all. God, did I feel like a prat—and a tart!

He helped me look for it, brushing up against me at the same time.

'Found it!' he yelled, slightly out of breath from diving in and out of the water. He helped me fasten it behind my back.

I thanked him shyly and then we swam for a while. As I began to tire, he gave me a hand out of the water, but we'd swum so far that we couldn't see Gwen and Brad anymore.

'That's okay, if we just walk back along the water's edge, we'll see them,' he said.

'So, are you enjoying your holiday, Ryan?' I asked, but then remembered he'd literally only just arrived. I stuttered, feeling like an idiot once again. It seemed to be happening rather a lot lately.

He laughed at my embarrassment. 'Of course, especially now that I've met you,' he replied, smiling and revealing his slightly crooked yet gleaming white teeth.

'Stop teasing,' I said at the same time as I stubbed my toe on a rock and nearly fell over. I grabbed onto him to stop the fall. 'Shit, bloody hell that hurt,' I gasped.

'Are you okay? Here, let's sit down for a second. Ooh, that looks a bit sore,' he said as he inspected my toe, which was bleeding. 'Here, dip it in the ocean. It'll sting a little, but it'll make it a whole lot better.'

What a sweet guy.

I hobbled with him to the sea. Sure enough, he was right; it hurt like hell. He obviously saw me wince because he put his arm around me and let me lean on him while we slowly walked along the shore.

'Thanks,' I said, hoping we could see a lot more of each other over the next couple of weeks.

'So, why don't you tell me about yourself, Summer Miller,' he questioned eagerly.

'I don't think you want to know about me. I'm just an ordinary girl with an ordinary life.'

'I don't believe a word of that for a second. You sure don't look like an ordinary girl to me.'

Smiling, I replied, 'Okay, but I'll soon change your mind. You'll soon see I'm ordinary, in every sense of the word.' I told him my age, where I lived and worked, all about the absence of a father during my life, what a wonderful boss I had (I just couldn't resist telling him about my mum and Jack).

He laughed and gasped at all the right times. 'You've told me all that but not once have you mentioned the men in your life. How come?' he asked.

'Well, that's probably because the men in my life have all been total losers. I had quite a long relationship with a guy called Russell, who I thought I wanted to marry and have babies with— until I found him in bed with my mother,' I laughed.

'Ouch! Now that must have been nasty.'

'It certainly was. It was not a pretty sight, I assure you. But I guess I've finally come to terms with it. Now my problem lies with another guy, who I've just finished with, but I really don't want to talk about that.'

Ryan clearly understood that to mean leave the subject well alone, so he didn't ask any more.

'Now it's your turn. I don't know anything about you,' I said as he smiled.

'Well, I'm thirty years old, and I live in Houston, Texas. Brad and I run a martial arts school there. It's great. We love it, we really do. It's something we've always wanted to do - ever since we were kids. Our students range from four to sixty years old, and they love it too. If you ever come to the States, I'd love to show it to you,' he said enthusiastically.

I smiled, knowing that he didn't really mean that. People always said that kind of thing when they were on holiday. It was a nice thought, though.

'I think the company where I work has a sister office in Houston. Isn't that where NASA is?'

'Yes, they do have a centre in Houston. It's a great place to live. In fact, the whole of Texas is a great place. There's so much to do. I absolutely love it there.'

'And the next question is: what about the women in your life?' I asked.

By the look on his face, I guessed it was a bit of a sore subject too.

'I was seeing someone for a few years, but she decided to move to Hollywood. She dreamed of becoming an actress, and I guess I was in her way, so she left. That was a couple of months ago. I haven't really dated anyone since.'

'I'm sorry to hear that. It's a pretty sad story. That is definitely her loss, though. Has she been in any movies or anything like that since she got there?'

'I don't think so. She doesn't keep in touch, so I guess I wouldn't really know if she had. But I'm getting to the stage where I really don't care. She left me, and that's that,' he said with just a little remorse.

'It won't be long until you've found someone new. A good looking man like yourself. It's a pity you live in the States,' I giggled.

'If that's a proposal, I might just take you up on that,' he laughed.

Neither of us had noticed that we'd walked right past Gwen and Brad. Only when we stopped to have a look back, did we see them waving at us. We waved back and headed back towards them.

I was having a great time, and it certainly had a lot to do with this gorgeous American hunk by my side.

'We called out to you guys, but you just walked straight past us,' chuckled Brad.

'Yeah? I think we were in a world of our own,' Ryan said as he looked down at me. I blushed and plonked myself down on my union jack towel.

Brad and Gwen looked at each other as if they thought something had been going on between us. We ignored it.

'We've had enough of the beach, for now, so we're gonna grab a drink in town. Do you want to come?' asked Brad as he and Gwen stood up to go.

'No, I'm going to stay here and get some more sun.'

'Yeah, me too,' said Ryan.

I smiled; I'd hoped he would say that.

The two left, saying they'd see us later at the hotels.

Ryan and I lay down quietly for a while, each in our own little world of thought. When I turned to look at him, he was lying on his side, watching me. I blushed and asked what he was doing.

'Just looking at a beautiful woman and thinking,' he answered.

'Thinking about what, exactly?'

'I was wondering what it would have been like if I'd have met you in Texas.'

'And what do you think it would have been like?'

'We'd be married by now with a little house and kids,' he laughed.

'Oh, really? You're pretty sure of yourself, aren't you?' I joked.

He tried to look hurt and said, 'You mean you don't agree with me? Don't you find me irresistible?'

I laughed at his expression as I told him he was the most irresistible man that I'd ever met. As I said it, he gently leaned over and kissed me softly on the lips but quickly pulled away and apologised. 'I'm sorry. I shouldn't have done that. I've only known you for about ten minutes.'

'Wow! You're s-s-sorry? Shit, don't be. Why are you sorry, anyway?'

'Well, we've literally only just met, and it was pretty stupid of me to assume you wanted to be kissed, I guess.'

'Ryan, believe me when I say I wanted to be kissed... By you, that is. It was great. Feel free to do it whenever you want,' I said, trying to make him laugh.

It worked. He leaned across to me again with a smile and kissed me again and again and again. 'Well, you said to do it whenever I want. Which means I'll be spending the next few weeks doing nothing but kissing you.'

I laughed and handed him the suntan lotion and asked if he

would mind rubbing some into my back. He said 'sure', in that gorgeous accent, and crawled even closer to me as I turned over. He carefully undid my bikini top and extremely gently rubbed the cream all over my back. It was so sensuously done that I could feel myself becoming more and more aroused, but I didn't want him to know, so I stayed where I was, whispering my thanks.

He lay back down on his towel and reached over for my hand. He squeezed it tightly. My stomach did a giant somersault. I can honestly say that I'd never quite felt like it before. I felt as if I'd known him for ages. It was weird.

Ryan had easily managed to get rid of all my awful memories from the past week or so. He made me feel like a beautiful woman. Just my luck that he lived in Texas, wasn't it? Bloody typical.

'I hope you'll let Brad and I take you and Gwen out for dinner tonight?' he suddenly said.

'That would be really nice. I'll look forward to it. Come to think of it, it's almost six-thirty already. We should really head back to the hotel. Brad's probably waiting for you there, I'm sure Gwen will be waiting for me,' I replied, hopping up and shaking out my towel.

We strolled back up the beach, not really wanting the day to end. Sure enough, when we got to the hotel, Gwen and Brad were waiting. Ryan told them of our plans for the evening, and we arranged to meet at 19h30.

Ryan gently kissed me on the cheek and waved goodbye. 'See y'all at half seven, then.'

My insides danced.

Gwen hardly said a word until we got up to our room. 'You've fallen for him really bad, haven't you?' she questioned.

'Oh, don't be silly. I hardly know the guy. We've only just met. Plus he lives in America, so what's the point?' But Gwen seemed to know me better than I knew myself sometimes, so I fell onto my bed and said, 'Okay, maybe I have, but what the hell can I do about it? Nothing. Absolutely bloody nothing. What is it with men and me for God's sake?'

'Well, Brad told me something you'd be interested in.'

'Yeah, what?'

'He said that he's known Ryan since they were really young, and he has never ever seen him react the way he reacted when he saw you. Brad was amazed at the effect you've had on his hunky friend. In fact, Brad is willing to bet that Ryan is gonna want to spend the next couple of weeks with you and just you. So what do you make of that, then?'

'Are you serious? You're not having me on, aren't you?'

She shook her head, vehemently.

'But what if we really do hit it off? What happens at the end of the holiday? He lives in Texas, and I live in London, for God's sake. Just a bit far for romance, wouldn't you think?' I said, but I smiled all the same.

She shrugged as she undressed, ready to hop into the shower.

'Don't take too long in the there, Gwen Pursehouse, I know what you're like in the bloody shower. Just remember I need to do a bit of beautifying too, y'know!' Okay, so I needed to do a bit more than just a bit.

'Nag, nag, nag, nag, nag!' she yelled back.

oOo

At 19h30, we were all dolled up and ready for a great night out with the American boys. And when we walked outside, we found they were patiently waiting for us.

'Howdy! Wow! Y'all look stunning!' they said, with wolf whistles all around. 'We'll be the envy of many a man in Praia da Rocha this evenin' for sure.'

Ryan kissed me gently on the cheek and whispered into my ear, 'You look like a princess. I hope I can be your Prince Charmin'.'

I told him I would be honoured and he held my hand as the four of us walked to the restaurant where they'd booked a table. It was a costly and luxurious place where the steaks were sinfully delicious, the wine divine and the company intoxicating. I never wanted to leave.

After dessert, while we had coffee and liquor, Ryan mentioned that he wanted to visit one of the big waterparks during their holiday, as well as do a bit of sight-seeing. 'I hope the two of you will come with us.'

'I think that sounds like a terrific idea. I'm game, and I know for a fact that little Summer here, is game too,' Gwen said, giggling, as I jokingly gave her leg a kick under the table.

The rest of the evening was an absolute blast. We spent much of the time bar-hopping and disco-diving. Ryan proved himself to be quite a dancer, and I noticed a hell of a lot of women ogling and drooling over him. Well, at least for the next two weeks, he'd made it quite clear that he was mine. All mine. Wow, he certainly was the sexiest man around. I was such a lucky girl.

Towards the end of the evening, or should I say morning, the four of us grabbed some towels from the hotel and went down to the beach to watch the stars until dawn. It was one of the most amazing nights of my life. We discussed which star was which, counted at least seventy shooting stars, and spent much of the night making wishes. Mine mostly consisted of highly unlikely things, like Ryan asking me to go back to Texas with him, Ryan proposing marriage, Ryan asking me to be the mother of his children, et cetera, et cetera. I was obviously totally pissed or something. I mean, me...want to settle down and have kids? Not bloody likely. Or...was it?

When the sun began to appear, we headed back, got showered and dressed and then met up for breakfast. We figured we'd get some sleep on the beach later. Absolutely and totally famished, we managed to find a nice English bar, which served proper full English breakfasts. Precisely what my stomach was grumbling for.

'I'm warning you, boys. This is not a healthy breakfast. It's not good for your lean and fit bodies,' I explained, laughing, but they were ready and willing to give it a go and try it out. Surely they must have had it before, anyway?

As it turned out, they thought the mixture of bacon, eggs, sausages, beans, tomatoes, mushrooms, toast and fried bread was excellent.

'We sure didn't know what we've been missing all these years,' they exclaimed, polishing off their meals and our leftovers too; not that I had much left over. God, what a pig.

But, as Gwen rightly put it, 'You sure as hell wouldn't have those sexy bodies if you'd had these breakfasts every day for the last twenty odd years.'

'Well, it's a delicious brekkie every once in a while,' I interrupted.

Entirely and utterly knackered after the sleepless night, we headed down to the beach for a nice long nap and some more sun and sea.

But after an hour or so, Gwen began complaining of pains in her stomach and lower back.

'Is it your period?' I asked while the boys had a dip in the sea.

'No,' she whispered. 'I don't know what it is, but it's getting worse.'

'Do you want to go back to the hotel?'

Gwen shook her head, 'Maybe just give it half an hour and see,' she said, rubbing her tummy.

But the pains began to gradually get worse and worse until she could hardly move. In fact, they became so bad that she began to cry from the pain.

'Summer, something is really wrong. I'm really scared,' she whispered, as she tried to stand up but immediately doubled over in agony. I was suddenly petrified for her; I had no idea what was wrong. I wasn't exactly known for my first aid skills.

'We need to get her to a hospital—fast,' said an anxious Brad as he and Ryan stood up.

'Can you two carry her?' I asked.

They slowly picked her up, careful not to make the pain any worse than it already was, while I ran up the beach to a bar to try and get some kind of help.

There were a few people drinking coffees and just one man behind the bar. I hoped he spoke English. 'Please, can you telephone for an ambulance? There is something wrong with my friend. I don't know what's wrong,' I cried, panicking, as tears slid down my cheeks.

Fortunately, he understood me perfectly and saw the distress in my face, so he immediately dialled for an ambulance, and offered to help in some way, as he tried to calm me down.

There were quite a few steps to climb, so he kindly offered to help Brad and Ryan carry her up. 'You run to the top, so the ambulance knows where to stop, okay? Don't worry, your friend will be just fine. We will look after her,' he said as they struggled with Gwen, who was almost howling in pain.

I'd never experienced anything like that before, and I was terrified. All I could think of was 'Gwen's going to die, my best friend's going to die'.

Finally, the ambulance arrived, and Gwen was strapped in. I asked to go with her, and the boys said they'd get a cab to follow us. I held her hand tightly and noticed her face had turned completely white. 'Please, do you know what's wrong?' I cried to the ambulance men.

'I'm sorry, madam, but you must wait until we reach the hospital,' he said without a shred of understanding. Arsehole. Okay, maybe not an arsehole, but he could have at least made an effort.

'Gwen? Gwen? It won't be long. You'll be fine. Okay, sweetheart? Don't worry. I'm right here. I'll be right here if you need me, okay?' My attempts to sound confident and comforting failed miserably. It was difficult to know if she could hear me or not because she simply couldn't speak.

At the hospital, she was taken in immediately, but I wasn't allowed in the ward with her. So I waited for Brad and Ryan, who arrived a couple of minutes later. Ryan rushed straight up to me and put his arms around me.

'Don't worry, she's going to be okay, baby. Shhh. She'll be fine,' he reassured me, kissing the top of my head. He actually helped me to calm down. I felt more at ease and was sure that, whatever was wrong, Gwen was going to pull through.

Every now and again, a nurse appeared, and every time I rushed up to ask if they knew anything about my English friend. They all gave me the same blank look.

I kept getting the same reply, 'Não falo Inglês,' and a shake of the head.

'There must be someone here who speaks English, for God's

sake,' I yelled in the corridor, as Ryan and Brad tried to calm me down again.

'Excuse me, madam. Can I help? I speak English?' said a sweet young woman with a baby who walked into the waiting room.

'Thank you, oh, thank you,' I said as I explained what had happened and that I just wanted to know if Gwen was alright or not. She said she would try and find out for me before she disappeared down another corridor.

Just five minutes later, she came back with someone who appeared to be a doctor.

'This doctor will help you, okay?' she said with a smile as she went to sit down. I thanked her profusely and asked the doctor if he knew about Gwen.

'Are you a relative of the young lady admitted an hour ago?' His English was perfect.

I said no, but I was her best friend, explaining that we were on holiday together.

'And the father of the baby?' he said, looking at Ryan and Brad.

Baby? What on Earth was he going on about? Gwen wasn't pregnant.

'What? What baby?' I stood utterly still with shock. 'You mean… You mean Gwen is—was—pregnant? Oh, my God. Oh my God!' Tears welled up in my eyes. Jesus. Gwen had been pregnant, and she'd lost it. I felt so guilty; she'd probably have been fine if I hadn't convinced her to come on holiday with me. Oh God, if only I'd known.

Ryan and Brad stood on either side of me and held me upright.

'Your friend is pregnant, madam, but she very nearly lost the baby. She is lucky. Very lucky.'

I nearly fell over again. 'Gwen is pregnant? Are you certain about that? She's alright? And the baby's alright? Can I see her?' I blurted.

'She and the baby will be fine. I will let you see her, but only for a minute. Then you must leave her. She will need to remain here for a few days, to regain her strength, okay? She must rest, for her and the baby's sake.'

I nodded and began to follow him. But first, I turned to Ryan and kissed him. 'I'll be right back.'

He squeezed my hand, and I turned to follow the doctor into Gwen's room; she wasn't alone in there, though. There were at least five other beds, all with ghastly-looking women in them.

Gwen was so pale. She didn't look like her usual bright self at all. As I approached the bed, she slowly opened her eyes. The corners of her mouth turned into as much of a smile as she could muster.

'Hi honey,' I whispered.

'Hey you,' she croaked, 'I guess you know about the baby.'

I nodded and held her hand, 'The baby's fine, and you're going to be fine too. A bit of shock to the system though, huh?'

She laughed slightly. 'Hugh?'

'I'll call him as soon as I can, okay. I'll tell him everything is going to be alright,' I promised.

'Will you tell him he's going to be a father? Will you…will you tell him…tell him, that, that I'll marry him?'

Tears rolled down my cheeks. She wanted me to tell him? 'Wouldn't you rather tell him yourself?' I asked, unsure why she wanted me to tell him the news.

'Please tell him, Summer. I'm in no state to…to… use a… telephone. He'll… he'll want to know. And Summer?'

'Yes, sweetheart?'

'Will you… be my… maid of honour?' She smiled again.

'Please, madam, she needs to rest now,' said the doctor behind me.

'Gwen, it would be my honour. Thank you for asking me… I have to go now, though. I promise to tell Hugh, okay?'

She nodded as I gently kissed her forehead, and then I followed the doctor back out to the waiting room, where Ryan and Brad stood, patiently waiting for me.

'Is she okay, Summer?' Brad asked. Ryan already knew from the look on my face.

'She's going to be fine. She's a bit weak, though. And I can't believe this, but she's going to have a baby. Oh, and she's decided to marry Hugh. I have to call him. I need to get back to the hotel. His phone number is there. You will come with me, won't you?'

They looked at me as if I was silly or something. 'Of course, we will.'

We weren't keen on leaving Gwen, but there was nothing else we could do. So, before we left, we checked when visiting hours were, so we could go back again later.

Back at the hotel, Brad and Ryan sat in the lobby while I went up to the room to make the call. God, I was totally exhausted. I found Gwen's mobile, which she'd been keeping at the hotel, and looked up Hugh's home and work numbers. It was one o'clock, so he'd probably be at work. He was a chiropractor and had his own little practice just outside London.

It rang for a little while before he answered. I figured his assistant and receptionist must have literally just left for lunch.

'Johnson's Chiropractic Clinic. Can I help you?'

'Hugh, is that you?'

'Yes, who's calling?

'Hugh, it's me, Summer.'

'Summer, what on Earth are you doing ca... Oh, my God. There's something wrong, isn't there? Is it Gwen. Is she alright?'

'Hugh, there's absolutely no need to panic...not now, anyway. Gwen is going to be fine. But she's in hospital.' I could hear him gasp on the other end of the line. I felt awful for him; I knew he'd desperately want to be here with her. I continued, 'But please don't worry. She collapsed on the beach this morning with terrible pains in her lower back and stomach. But she's going to be okay. They're keeping her in for a few days for observation and rest.' I could hear him breathe a sigh of relief. 'There's something else, Hugh.'

'What? What is it? Tell me, Summer, please.'

'If you're not sitting down, you'd better sit down now. This is going to be a bit of a shock.'

'Oh, God, she hasn't got some terminal illness or something has she?'

Despite myself, I smiled. 'Hugh, you're going to be a father.'

I heard some kind of crash at the other end.

'Hugh? Hugh? Hello? Hugh? Are you there? Are you alright? I did tell you to sit down, didn't I?' I laughed.

'I'm here. I'm okay. I'm going to be a dad? I can't believe it!' He whooped with joy.

'Er, Hugh, there's more...'

'What?'

'I told Gwen she should tell you herself, but for some reason she wanted me to tell you...'

'Oh, God. What more could there be?'

'Hugh, she wants to marry you,' I said with a huge grin from ear to ear.

'Oh, God. Are you sure she said that to you? Really?'

'Of course, why else would I say it if she hadn't told me?'

I could tell he was jumping for joy. He was completely ecstatic by the sounds of things.

'Summer, I'm getting on the first plane over. If I can get one today, I'll see you later, okay? Don't worry about meeting me at the airport, I'll manage.'

So I gave him the details of the hotel, and everything else he needed to know and told him I was really looking forward to seeing him. 'Gwen is going to have a serious shock when you turn up,' I said before putting the phone down.

I was thrilled. My best friend was getting married and having a baby, and I had been the bearer of the wonderful news to her other half, who was completely and utterly ecstatic. I felt good. In fact, apart from the fact that Gwen was still stuck in that horrible hospital, I felt terrific. And to complete the package was the fact that the sexiest man alive was downstairs waiting for me.

My God—for someone who thought life was a bitch last week, I sure had changed my tune. Life was fantastic, and I was living it to the full. Yeeehaaaa!

CHAPTER 8

'Are you sure you're okay?' asked Hugh, concern written all over his face.

'Oh, for God's sake. Yes, I feel exactly like I did ten minutes ago when you asked me the exact same question. Darlin', I'm fine. There's absolutely no need to mother me,' replied Gwen as she squeezed his hand.

I was so happy for them. Hugh had managed to get a flight the day after Gwen had been admitted to hospital. She hadn't known about it. I didn't tell her that he'd said he was flying over; I thought she deserved a surprise. Not that she hadn't had enough of those in the last couple of days.

Brad, Ryan and I had visited her at the hospital and stayed until we were literally kicked out by a big butch nurse—not someone to mess with, believe me. And besides, when Hugh had arrived, he'd made it quite clear that he would look after her. Both he and Gwen had told me to go and enjoy my time with Ryan. After all, we only had a little over a week left together.

Outside Gwen's hospital room, Hugh had thanked us for taking care of her and for being there when she'd needed us the most. 'Summer, you're a true friend to Gwen, and I'm so pleased that she wants you to be her maid of honour. Gwen told me that she considers you to be the sister she never had, which means you're going to be my sister-in-law,' he'd said with a hug. I was so touched, I actually cried.

When she'd been released, later that same day on Thursday, I'd assumed Hugh would take her straight back home to England, but when I brought up the subject, she'd looked at me as if I was completely mad, or worse. 'No way. I'm not going back to freezing cold England. And Hugh is here to look after me now. We can enjoy the rest of the holiday together,' she'd said with a loving smile in his direction, as she'd gently rubbed her tummy.

'I still can't believe I'm going to be a mum,' she'd whispered shyly, happiness personified.

I must admit, I'd been really concerned at first, but she was soon back to her usual self. I breathed a sigh of relief.

oOo

ON FRIDAY, we all sat on the beach, enjoying the scorching sun. All four of us were continually pampering the newly-found-to-be-pregnant Gwen, who was basking in all the attention, proud to be in the limelight for all the right reasons.

Ryan suddenly jumped up and asked me if I would join him for a swim. He helped me up, and we wandered down to the water. It was still freezing, but we didn't care; we were just happy to be together and that Gwen was alright.

He dived in as I slowly walked in, gradually adjusting my body to the cold temperature, but he began splashing me, so I soon immersed myself totally. What a rush.

We joked around for a while, ducking each other beneath the water and splashing one another until we were breathless, then we calmed down and swam a couple of hundred metres until we could no longer see our friends on the beach.

I'd never had so much fun in my entire life. Here I was, in a beautiful warm country, with my pregnant best friend and this totally gorgeous bloke by my side. During the last couple of days, not once had I thought of the shit job back home, Mr Negativity, my unusually tarty mother or the He-Whore. I really felt as if I was in another world. I sure as hell never wanted this to end. I pushed the fact that it was going to in a week to the recesses of my mind. Definitely, not something I wanted to think about.

'I'll bet you're thinkin' exactly what I'm thinkin,' Ryan said, as he swam close beside me.

'And exactly what are you thinking?'

'That I'm having the time of my life. That I don't want this to end.'

'Wow. You must be a mind reader or something. They were my thoughts exactly,' I said, thinking we were definitely on the same wavelength.

He smiled, and my heart skipped a beat, or rather a couple of thousand.

'How about tomorrow we go to the waterslide park? You said the other day that you wanted to go, but in light of recent events, it hasn't really been possible. What do you reckon?' I asked.

'That'd be fabulous. Let's go ask the others, shall we?'

Ryan helped me out of the water, and we went and asked what they thought of the idea. Hugh was a bit concerned about Gwen going on the slides. 'I don't think it's such a great idea, Gwen really should be resting.'

'I don't have to go on the slides, do I? Yeah, I think it'd be great. I'm more than happy to just sit and watch you guys and catch some rays,' she suggested happily.

'Are you sure? Wouldn't it be a bit boring for you?' asked Brad.

She shook her head, vigorously. 'I'll be fine. Will you all stop worrying about me, and enjoy yourselves for a change? Honestly, you'd think I was on my deathbed or something. So that's it. Tomorrow we go sliding, whether you like or not, Mr Johnson,' she teased.

I felt a bit guilty for causing problems, but Ryan soon made me feel better. All he had to do was smile, and I turned into jelly—a mountain of it.

oOo

THE NEXT DAY, we rented a big car and drove to the waterpark first thing in the morning. We were amongst the first people there, which meant we could use most of the slides before the queues began. By the afternoon, we had to wait fifteen or twenty minutes to go on each one, but it was worth it. We were having a brilliant time. Even Gwen found a great spot in one of the calmer swimming pools, where she spent the majority of the day, and we all spent time with her at some point or other.

Ryan, Brad and Hugh were like three big kids, running from one slide to another, and talking excitedly about each one.

'Wow, that was awesome, come and try this one, Summer. You'll love it!' That was all I heard all day. Mind you, I suppose I was just as enthusiastic, until on one of the slides I managed to hurt my back, so I thought I'd better slow down for a while. It had been one of those with a massive drop at the bottom, into a very very deep pool. Not only had it hurt my back, but it had also given me one serious wedgie, which bloody hurt my bum. So, feeling sorry for myself, I went and sat down to give my bum and back a much-needed rest.

Soon Ryan realised I was sitting alone on my towel, so he came and joined me. 'Somethin' wrong, honey?' he asked, as he took my hand in his and kissed it gently.

I loved it when he called me that. 'No, I'm okay really, just hurt my back a little bit on the drop slide. It's nothing, really,' I smiled.

'Here, let me rub it for you.' He sat behind me and gave me the most fantastic back massage. 'How's that? Good?' he asked.

'Wow, Ryan, mmmm, that's amazing,' I said, my eyes closed in bliss.

He explained that he and Brad were both qualified masseurs; apparently, it went with the job of teaching martial arts because sometimes people got hurt.

Wow, was there anything this man couldn't do? It was certainly a turn-on.

Ryan and I hadn't slept together. It wasn't that we hadn't wanted to, it was just that neither of us wanted to rush into anything and we wanted each other to know how much we respected each other. It wasn't about sex. Well, okay, I admit, it was at first. That was all I'd wanted, but as I got to know him, the feeling changed. We didn't need sex to have fun, anyway. That was something I was slowly learning. In my other relationships, perhaps that was where I'd gone wrong. I'd always jumped into the sack at the very first opportunity. Sex had always been the most essential thing before. Whereas really, you should get to know the person properly first. Something I'd never really understood. My mum hadn't exactly been a good role model in that respect.

'What are you thinking about, sweet stuff?'

I just loved it when he called me those sweet lovey-dovey names. It was ever so adorable. 'Nothing, really, just respect and sex, friendship and stuff,' I muttered under my breath.

He laughed. 'You don't have to mutter that kind of stuff, you know, it's perfectly natural. Sex, that is,' he joked louder so that everyone around could hear.

I went a bit red because, just as he'd thought, everybody looked at us at the first mention of the word. People really were prudish, including me, by the looks of things.

He just chuckled and kissed me as he finished rubbing my back. 'Is that better?'

'Absolutely.' I didn't mention my sore bum, though.

'So, you gonna come on another slide with me, then?' he asked, like a little kid. I couldn't resist his charm, so I got up and joined him on the rings.

At 5.30 we noticed people were beginning to leave and realised we'd been having so much fun we'd forgotten to eat.

'I don't know about you guys, but I'm starving!' announced Brad.

'I sure am, too,' said Ryan, as the rest of us nodded profusely.

'Okay then, let's head back, get cleaned up, and go out for dinner,' I said, as we picked up our towels and bags and headed out of the park.

oOo

WHEN HUGH HAD FIRST ARRIVED in Praia da Rocha, he'd been fortunate in managing to get a room in our hotel, which meant Gwen had moved in with him and I had a room to myself. I did miss her company, though.

However, it meant that I was able to get ready in record time, so Brad and Ryan often came up to my room to wait for the lovebirds. This time they brought a bottle of wine with them, so we had a drink on the terrace while we waited.

Brad said he felt a bit of a gooseberry, but we reassured him that he was nothing of the sort. We really enjoyed his company and tried to make him feel completely comfortable and at ease with us. He was obviously looking forward to getting back home to Cherry, his fiancee back home, though, and the fact that he was spending so much time with two couples didn't help.

'Do you miss Cherry, Brad?' I asked him that evening.

The look on his face clearly said yes, and he nodded enthusiastically. 'I've actually been calling her every day,' he said with a smile.

Aw, that's so sweet, I thought.

Finally, there was a knock at the door, and Hugh and Gwen arrived, all dressed up and ready for the off. 'Okay, folks, so where are we off to tonight then?'

'I noticed a great looking restaurant down by the beach. Fancy giving it a try?' said Hugh.

We all agreed and walked down to it. It was jam-packed, but the waiter told us that if we were willing to wait half an hour, and have a drink at the bar first, a table would soon become available. We took him up on the offer, and Brad decided to go call Cherry again. He really did miss her. He'd realised that it was probably not the best of times to make a phone call to her, but he was desperate to hear her voice.

'He really is smitten with this girl, isn't he?' I asked Ryan. 'How long have they been together?'

'She's a great girl. They've actually been together since high school. Neither of them has ever been with anyone else. I think that's kinda cool. They must be soulmates, they're so lucky to have found each other,' he said, smiling, but with a sad glint in his eye.

I put my hand to his cheek and told him he'd find his soulmate in the States one day.

'Maybe I've already found her,' he said quietly as he squeezed my hand and looked deep into my eyes. I really wished it could work, but deep down I knew it couldn't.

I shook my head. 'As much as I'd love to be her, it's impossible, Ryan. We live in different countries. On different continents, for that matter. It would never work.' I realised I was actually trying to convince myself of that too.

'Let's not even think about it. We've got less than a week together, why don't we enjoy the time that we do have, hey? Let's be happy, not sad. We're having a super time here.'

But inside, my heart sank. I was falling in love with him, and I knew we couldn't have a relationship. Not living on opposite sides of the world.

Ryan looked sad but put on a brave face for me. He kissed me softly on the lips, just as Brad walked back in. He was smiling.

'You obviously got through, then?' asked Ryan.

'Yup. She's great, but she misses me like crazy.'

I tried to figure out why he took a holiday without her if he felt so madly in love with her, but couldn't work it out, so I asked him when Ryan went to the loo.

'Simply because of Ryan. He thought it would be a good idea for the two us to have a break. I guess he's worried he's gonna lose his best friend when I get married, which really isn't going to happen... Now that we're here, I think it's all down to fate. Fate brought us here to meet you. I've never seen Ryan act like this before. I think he's finally found love. With you.' He stopped talking abruptly as Ryan came and sat back down with us.

'My, why the sad faces?'

I quickly changed the subject but smiled at Brad, a kind of thank-you for telling me his thoughts. But it didn't change the fact that it simply wouldn't work.

Hugh and Gwen hadn't heard a word of what we'd been talking about; they were in their own little world of weddings and babies, which was incredibly cute. They looked so in love, and they had so much going for them. I was so envious. Deep down, I knew that I wanted to have what they shared.

The waiter soon called us over to a table by an open window, with magnificent views of the ocean, where we sat and ate the most sumptuous meal. It was utterly delightful.

oOo

THE NEXT DAY, considering we still had the use of the hire car, we decided to go up to the west coast. Apparently, it was a great place to watch the surfers strut their stuff, and the beaches were beautiful. So we popped into a local supermarket and bought plenty of food and drink for lunch, and piled into the car to begin our journey.

We'd been told to head to Sagres first, to check out the lighthouse and fortress. We had been reliably informed it was the most south-westerly point of Europe, so we figured we should give it a look-see. Ryan drove, with Brad sat beside him, and I sat in the back with the two love-birds. It was a beautiful hot day, and we were all grateful for the air conditioning!

When we arrived, we had a wander around for half an hour and stopped for a quick coffee so Gwen could use the loo, which she seemed to be doing an awful lot of lately. Then we piled back into the car and headed for Carrapateira: the beach that had come highly recommended by the hotel receptionist.

An hour later we were driving down a dusty road just off the main road, following the signs for praia—the beach. When we first glimpsed the beach and the ocean, we soon realised why it had been so highly recommended. It was absolutely beautiful. Unfortunately, as it was a Sunday, it was very crowded. But we soon found a place to park and then carried everything down to a suitable spot.

We sat down and admired the breath-taking view around us. The waves were fairly big, but not huge, and a few surfers were strutting their stuff and posing for the girls.

Ryan and Brad tried to get me to go in the sea with them, but I'd obviously neglected to tell them about my fear of the waves.

'Aw, c'mon, Summer, you'll be alright. I'll protect ya!'

I shook my head profusely. 'Sorry, guys, there's no way in hell you're gonna get me in the sea today. Not unless the waves die down and it's dead calm. Otherwise, no way.'

They shrugged their shoulders and asked Hugh if he fancied a swim. He nodded and got up, giving Gwen a quick peck on the cheek before they ran towards the water like a group of kids.

'So, finally…a little bit of time to ourselves. I've wanted to talk to you for a while, but it's been a bit tough with Hugh—and Ryan —around.' She smiled.

'Yeah, I know. So, what's on your mind?'

'I just thought it'd be nice to have a bit of a girlie chat, for a change. Plus, I haven't really had a chance to talk to you about anything, the baby or the wedding. I mean, I haven't even told you when the baby is due, have I?'

'I've meant to ask, but I didn't want to interfere between you and Hugh. I hope you know how unbelievably happy and thrilled I am for you. So, when is this miniature Gwen gonna be appearing into our lives? Huh?'

Laughing, she told me that the doctor had told her she was four months pregnant. 'It's due on November 20th. And we've decided to get married as soon as possible. So I think we've pretty much decided to set a date for the wedding on August 25th.'

'That's great. It's so exciting. Oh, God, I'm so happy,' I said as I jumped up and went over to give her a big hug.

She looked sad for a second as she said she wished her parents were alive to be there and meet their grandchild. 'They'd be so happy, I know they would'.

'Of course they would. But they will be there. They'll be there in spirit. Have you decided who is going to give you away?'

'I'm going to ask my grandad if he will do it.'

I told her I thought he'd be over the moon, and we chuckled like schoolgirls.

'So, what's going on with you and Ryan, then?'

I explained everything. The fact that we were probably getting too involved, that Brad said he reckoned it was fate that brought them to the Algarve at the same time as us, and that Ryan was beginning to think we were soulmates.

'But that's great, Summer. So why the sad face?'

'It won't work. In fact, I've already decided that I'm not going to keep his contact details, and I won't give him mine. I haven't told him yet, though. I've had too many broken relationships to go through another one. I just couldn't bear it again.'

Gwen said she understood. 'Well, you know I'm always here for you, and if that's your decision, then I'll stand by you. I do understand.'

I smiled and squeezed her hand as we watched the boys do a bit of unsuccessful body surfing. We laughed and giggled at them, making total fools of themselves. I took the camera from my bag, and we walked down to the water's edge to take photos of them fooling around.

When they saw us, they waved and tried to convince us to join them, but we said no and went back to lie on the towels in the sun.

About half an hour later they finally emerged from the sea, but much to our shock, they'd found an old kids' bucket, which they'd filled with freezing cold water and proceeded to tip it all over us.

'Aaaaaaargh!' we screamed.

I jumped up. 'I'm gonna get you for that, Ryan!' and I chased him all over the beach until I was exhausted, never quite managing to grab hold of him. He was way too fast for me, and he kept dodging me from one side to the other. He laughed and shook his head as I gave up and headed back to the others, who were laughing at the two of us.

'Well, you lot try and get him! He's bloody fast!' I chuckled. 'I don't know about you guys, but I've certainly worked up an appetite. I'm starving.' They seemed to be looking at something going on behind me, and before I knew it, Ryan had found a giant piece of seaweed and had placed it on my head. I left it there, acting totally normal. 'Well, Ryan's found my lunch, what are you guys having?' I laughed.

I finally threw it back at him, and he threw it at Brad, who threw it at Hugh, who was too nice to throw it at Gwen, so we sat down and took the food out of the cooler bag.

'Who fancies a beer, then?' asked Hugh.

An hour later, we'd eaten all of the sandwiches and crisps, and we'd all had a couple of beers, except Gwen, who had stuck to orange juice. She'd decided to stop drinking alcohol, not wanting to harm the baby any more than she may have already done, or so she thought. We all lay down and had a nap, Ryan with his arm in mine, Hugh stroking Gwen's belly and Brad smiling, obviously dreaming about Cherry.

We stayed on the beach until about 5.30 before packing up and strolling back up the beach towards the car. We got back to Praia da Rocha just before seven, after a leisurely drive back.

Hugh and Gwen decided to spend the evening at the hotel, so it was just Brad, Ryan and me. We hadn't been down to the marina yet, so we figured we'd go there for pizza and then check out the local bars. We'd bumped into Lisa and Amy when we'd got back from the beach, and they'd said it was a great place to go.

They were right. It was a super place. We went to an Italian restaurant for pizza and then wandered around looking at the boats for half an hour before we found a trendy bar, where we spent the rest of the evening talking to a group of Australians who were spending the summer in the Algarve doing a bit of work here and there. They were a fun group of five girls and three blokes. The girls were so drop-dead gorgeous you'd have thought they were models, and so were the blokes, come to think of it. I was astonished that Ryan still managed to have eyes only for me. So surprised, in fact, that I actually asked him about it.

'What do you think of the Australians then, Ryan?'

'They sure are a blast.'

'Don't you find them attractive?'

'Sure, they're very pretty. But they don't have anything on you, Summer,' he said with a sexy smile and a wink.

I went weak at the knees. I couldn't believe it. How could he possibly think that? I mean, yeah, I was quite tall and thin, but I had cropped blonde hair, ordinary features and dull green eyes. I'd never considered myself to be a looker. Yeah, a couple of people had said they thought I was pretty, but I'd never taken any notice of them. Mind you, I supposed Ryan could just be saying that to keep me happy, couldn't he? God, I was so negative. If Gwen had been with me, she'd have moaned about my lack of self-esteem.

'You're a gorgeous girl, Summer, why can't you see that?' was what she'd say. I suppose I should give myself a chance, shouldn't I?

Brad and Ryan had really clicked with the Aussie blokes, probably because they were interested in martial arts too. They swapped email addresses just before we left, saying that if they were ever in the States, they should make a point of visiting.

Then we said our goodbyes and left them to it, and the boys walked me to the lobby of my hotel and arranged to come by the next morning.

oOo

THE FOLLOWING day we decided to head into the nearby town of Portimão to do a spot of shopping. We started off as a group but soon split up. Hugh and Gwen went to do the baby thing, leaving Brad, Ryan and myself to our own devices. But before we went our separate ways we found a local Portuguese coffee shop and each had agalão—milky coffee in a glass—and atosta mista—ham and cheese toastie—which were very tasty. We agreed to meet up at one o'clock for lunch, considering that was when the shops shut for a couple of hours.

'Are you looking for anything in particular?' Brad asked me.

'I don't think so. Something for my mum, I s'pose... Oh, and something for Gwen's baby. Mind you, I don't know if it's going to be a boy or a girl, but I guess that really doesn't matter. How about you? Actually, I already know the answer to that question. You're looking for something for Cherry, right?'

He blushed and said yes, along with something for his 'folks'.

Ryan said pretty much the same thing.

So we wandered around, but every now and again we were approached by gipsies, who seemed to think Ryan and Brad wanted to buy 'very very cheap gold watches'. When we shook our heads, the gipsies said, 'Hash, you want hash,senhor?'

'Do we look like we're into drugs or something?' asked Ryan, throwing his arms up in the air in annoyance, although he did eventually see the funny side.

'Just ignore them, sweetheart.'

Sweetheart? Where on Earth had that come from? He obviously liked me calling him that, though, because he smiled and squeezed my hand.

I couldn't find the right thing for my mother, so I settled for a tablecloth, which I managed to barter down from fifty euros to thirty from a local gipsy. I'm sure my mother would hate it, but what do you buy a woman like that? Naughty knickers or something? I wasn't going to encourage her! I also decided to buy a little gift for Jim at work, as it had been his idea for me to have a break, and he seemed to be my only pal there. I bought him a couple of bottles of wine and a funny but rather rude key ring. I was pretty sure he had a sense of humour.

For Gwen's baby, I saw the most adorable handmade booties that I couldn't resist, so I bought a pair in blue and a pair in white. They were so cute. I wanted to buy something else too, but couldn't decide what, so Ryan and Brad helped me choose a beautiful delicate handmade baby blanket in white and gold. It was the most exquisite thing I'd ever seen. It cost quite a bit, but it sure was worth it. I knew Gwen would cherish it.

Ryan and Brad had bought some wine and port for their fathers and a couple of pristine white lace tablecloths for their mothers. For Cherry, Brad had a lot of trouble finding the right thing, and I didn't have a clue what she was like, so I wasn't really much help. Ryan offered his assistance, and together they found a dazzlingly gorgeous gold necklace with an unusual stone in it. Brad seemed incredibly impressed with it, which was the most important thing. I popped into a boutique next door while they bought it, as they took absolutely ages finding the right one.

In this little boutique, I found a lovely little maternity dress. I had to buy it for Gwen because it was so cute. It was a stretch denim mini dress with tiny white flowers all over it. I knew she'd fall in love with it, so I didn't hesitate. I loved buying presents for friends; it was such a lot of fun.

When I came out of the shop, the boys were only just coming out of the jewellers. They were talking and smiling, but as soon as they spotted me, they shut up, almost as if they were hiding something.

'What's going on, you two?'

'Nothing. Don't know what you're talking about.' They both smiled, failing miserably at trying to look innocent. I shrugged my shoulders and gave up, and we walked on, but we soon realised it was already five to one, so we quickly headed towards the car, where Hugh and Gwen were already waiting. We put all our stuff inside and locked it back up again before heading towards the harbour where we'd been told we must try the sardines.

It was beginning to get busy, and the smell of the fish was divine.

'Mmm, I hadn't realised how hungry I was,' said Gwen.

'What? But you've been pigging out all morning,' exclaimed Hugh.

'Oh, give the poor girl a break, she's pregnant, she's allowed,' I smiled.

Everybody laughed as we found a table and ordered sardines all round with a bottle of white wine, for a change, to complement the fish.

It was extremely smoky where the sardines were being barbecued, and when we eventually left our eyes were streaming. We'd decided to do more shopping, only this time, us girls wanted to be on our own, so Gwen and I headed off, leaving the boys together.

'We'll meet you back at the car at five,' we said as we linked arms and headed back towards the shops.

'So, what did you buy this morning then?' I asked.

'Just a few things for the baby, and a couple of little things for my grandma and granddad. And you?'

'That's a secret.'

'Oh, do tell, Summer. Have you bought something for the baby too? You have, haven't you? I can tell by your face. Oh, that's so sweet. This kid is going to be spoilt rotten by you... and me and Hugh. But you don't have to, y'know.'

'I know that. But I want to. It's my prerogative. I'm your best friend.'

She smiled and thanked me as we headed into quite a trendy-looking boutique.

'This looks like a cool shop. I avoided going into places like these this morning, I didn't want to bore the boys.'

'Yeah, I know what you mean. But we can go mad now, can't we?' She giggled.

I picked up a little skin tight snakeskin-patterned mini dress. 'Here you go, Gwen, a couple more months and this will look stunning on you.' I held it up for her to see, and she nearly choked.

'Ooh, yeah, baby, yeah.'

It was clear she wasn't going to see anything suitable in there, and everything was a bit too tight for my liking, so we exited and walked into another store close by which looked a tad more hopeful. I found a really lovely black crochet bikini that I fell in love with, so I just had to have it, and Gwen found a sweet white blouse that would look great on her, especially when her bump was more significant.

During the next hour or so, we bought several more items of clothing, and I bought a great pink handbag and pink shoes, which Gwen encouraged me to get. 'Pink is great with your colouring, Summer. Go for it.' So I did.

I wanted to buy something for Ryan—so he wouldn't forget me and the great times we'd had—but wasn't sure what to get. 'What d'you reckon? It's tough buying something like that for a guy.'

'Guys wear bracelets and necklaces. In fact, a necklace would look great on Ryan. Mind you, it might get broken when he's teaching karate and stuff.'

'Exactly. Shit, there must be something I can get. How about a ring?'

'You don't know what size, do you?'

'Nope.'

'Well, you've still got time, we've still got a few days left. Why don't you think about it? That way, you might think of the perfect gift later.'

'You're such a star, Gwen. I don't know what I'd do without you, hon.'

She gave me a big hug. 'Well, you'll never get to know what it is like without me 'cos I'm always goin' to be around.'

Before we knew it, it was five o'clock, so we rushed back to the car. The boys weren't even there yet. Fortunately, I had the keys in my handbag, so we sat inside and turned on the air-con. Half an hour later, they finally arrived.

'Sorry we're late, we found this little arcade place, and we've been playing games for the past hour or so,' said Hugh.

We both tutted. 'Boys and their toys,' I said.

Ryan gave me a big apologetic kiss, just as Hugh did to Gwen, and Brad pretended to kiss some imaginary woman next to him, which made us all crack up with laughter.

'Good afternoon, ladies and gentleman, I'm your designated driver for the afternoon. Where would you like to go next?' Ryan said, in a desperate attempt at an English accent.

We cracked up again and told him his English accent needed some serious work.

He chuckled. 'Do you want to head back to Praia da Rocha or do you fancy going somewhere else for a change?'

'How about that lovely little town we saw on the coach, Summer?' Gwen suggested.

'We saw quite a few. Which one?'

'I can't remember its name. Wasn't it Praia do somewhere or other? Er, Praia do C…Creioro? No, Careiro? No, that wasn't it.'

'Praia do Carvoeiro?' said Hugh.

'That's it. How d'you know that?' I asked.

He held up a map, and we clapped him on the back.

'Clever boy, Hugh.'

'Okay, Praia do Carvoeiro here we come,' said Ryan, as we

drove slowly out of Portimão, amidst the heavy traffic.

Since Hugh had the map, he became the designated co-pilot and, I must say, he did do an excellent job, because twenty minutes later we were driving through the town looking for a parking space. It was pretty busy, and there didn't seem to be many spaces, so we kept on driving up through the town. We took a right turn and found ourselves on the most gorgeous cliff tops, signposted Algar Seco.

'Well, it looks like we can park here, guys,' said Ryan, driving into a space that became available seconds before.

'We can walk into town from here, I guess. Are you okay walking, Gwen?' Hugh asked.

'Of course I am, silly. I'm pregnant, not an invalid!'

He apologised as she playfully punched his arm.

I took out the camera and asked Brad if he'd take a photo of Ryan and me with the ocean behind us. Just as he was about to, Ryan grabbed me and pulled me towards him, planting a huge kiss on my lips. Brad snapped away.

'That should make a great picture!' he laughed, handing it back to me.

We began walking down the steep hill, taking a different road to the one we'd followed in the car, towards a very pretty small clifftop church.

'Now, there's a great little church for your wedding, Gwen.'

'Yeah, it's beautiful, isn't it? But we're definitely tying the knot in England. It's easier…and cheaper.'

We continued walking until we saw a little beach. We stopped and watched people swimming and generally enjoying themselves until Gwen spotted an ice cream parlour. 'I scream, you scream, we all scream for ice-cream,' she sang.

'Something tells me Gwen fancies an ice-cream,' I laughed, and we all decided to have one while walking around town.

'I want the biggest one they have,' she yelled after us as Ryan, and I ran down the hill, racing each other. Of course, Ryan reached the bottom first and held out his open arms so I could run straight into them, where he swung me around until I was dizzy.

'I'm having a great time, Summer,' he drawled as he slowed

down and pushed my overgrowing fringe from my eyes.

'Me too,' I answered as I, once again, turned to jelly, moving closer to him to kiss him hard on the lips.

By the time the others reached us, we were out of breath.

'Now, now, you two, stop trying to swallow each other,' exclaimed Gwen, and I turned crimson with embarrassment.

'Gwen!'

'Now, let's go get this ice cream,' she said, her eyes bulging as she saw people walking out of the parlour with huge cornets, piled high with ice cream and chantilly.

Hugh treated us all. Mine was just a small one, with mint-choc-chip ice cream, but Ryan had my other favourite—rum and raisin —so we swapped halfway through. Gwen had loads of different flavours, which she had to eat rather quickly as it began melting, dripping all over her fingers and her face.

'Gwen Pursehouse, anybody'd think you were a little kid trapped in a woman's body,' I laughed.

'Huh? I'm pregnant, so I'm allowed,' she said, sticking out her tongue at me.

We laughed at her as we walked, checking out the seemingly large number of restaurants and bars in the town. The only disco we saw was on the beach.

We decided that we'd hang around and have dinner there. But seeing as it was only late afternoon, and we'd just scoffed ice cream, we went to a local bar for a few drinks, where we sat and watched the world go by. We talked and talked about anything and everything until we realised it was half-past eight. We asked the barman for a recommendation of somewhere to eat dinner, and he kindly gave us a couple of ideas. We thanked him and walked up 'restaurant hill' until we came to one of the places he'd suggested, but it was jam-packed, as were the majority of the restaurants there.

'I guess we shouldn't have chatted for so long,' said Hugh.

'Oh, there's bound to be somewhere around here where we can eat,' replied Brad as we continued searching the numerous restau-rants until we found one where a group of people were just leaving.

'Aha, this looks like a table, here, folks. Shall we give it a try?'

We nodded in agreement and went in and sat down.

Once we placed our order of steak, which came recommended by the waiter, he brought bibs to the table for everyone.

'Don't you think we're a little old to be using bibs?' I joked.

In perfect English, he said, 'No. you're never too old for anything!' He laughed. 'Besides, these steaks are served raw on a hot stone, so you can cook them to your taste, which means they usually spit everywhere.'

Ah, well that explained it, then.

I smiled at him. 'Your English is excellent.'

'Thank you. But I guess it should be, considering I'm from Birmingham,' he laughed.

'Oh, well then, there you go,' I felt such a prat, but I suppose I should have known, considering his blonde hair and blue eyes and, of course, his accent.

When he left, Gwen laughed at me. 'You must feel like a right idiot, Summer.'

'You can say that again.'

'Summer, you must feel like a right idiot,' she said again, laughing.

Brad and Hugh were deep in conversation about their wedding plans, so Gwen began chatting to them.

Ryan leaned forward and said, 'You could never look like an idiot, babe,' before planting a big kiss on my lips. Of course, being a bit of a prude, I blushed—I wasn't exactly used to being snogged in the middle of restaurants.

When the steaks arrived, we concentrated hard on cooking them on the stones, and soon realised why we needed bibs. The juices from the meat kept splashing everywhere, and much to my annoyance I was the messiest one there—especially considering my comment about us being too old for bibs in the first place.

In fact, when we'd finished, the waiter commented on the mess I'd made. Cheeky bugger.

'And you thought I was the kid trapped in an adult's body,' grinned Gwen.

'Okay, okay. Ryan, I have to tell you the truth. I'm not a woman,

' I paused and tried to keep a straight face; his face was a picture. 'I'm actually a five-year-old, but I made a wish to be a grown-up, and it came true. Have you ever seen the film "Big", with Tom Hanks? Well, that's precisely what happened to me.' I tried so hard to look serious but I just couldn't; it was too funny.

'Well, darlin', the same thing happened to me, and I'm just six, so we can grow up together, okay?' he said, putting his thumb in his mouth and sucking it.

I howled with laughter, so much so that I got the funniest look from a pompous-looking woman who was obviously trying hard not to let the Chinese sex balls fall out of her hoohaa. Silly cow. Gwen saw too, so I whispered my thoughts to her, and we cracked up.

We paid the bill and went for a drink around the corner. It was actually a karaoke bar, so we didn't stay too long. It was too painful, and I wasn't drunk enough, so I sure as hell wasn't going to give it a go. I tried to get Ryan to get up for a singsong, but he wouldn't. I imagined he was probably like me; he'd sound like a cat in severe pain. We managed to get Brad up there, and his voice was like nothing I'd ever heard before. In fact, he sounded like a horny angel. Wow! Everybody in the bar went quiet; the women seemed to be in heaven, and the blokes were obviously impressed. He sang Right Here Waiting by Richard Marx, and he was bloody fantastic.

When he finished, the bar roared with whistles, clapping and shouting. People begged him to sing another one, so he did one more (Careless Whisper by George Michael) and then we left.

'My God, Brad, that was amazing. You should have been a singer. Wow. What a voice,' I said, amazed.

He was quite shy and wasn't sure how to take compliments, so he just blushed a little and said thank you.

'Y'know what you should do, Brad?' questioned Gwen, 'You should sing a song to Cherry at your wedding. That would be soooooo romantic.'

Brad shook his head in utter embarrassment. 'I don't think so.'

Then Ryan piped up, 'Actually, Brad, y'know, you should. It would be great. She'd be so surprised. It's a great idea. You should definitely give it some thought.'

On the way back to Praia da Rocha, we tried to get him to sing a song in the car, but he wouldn't. I guess he really was embarrassed. So, to give him a helping hand, I opened my mouth and belted out (quite painfully, I'm sure) Tomorrow from Annie. Everyone joined in, and we must have sounded awful together, but it was hilarious.

Why Tomorrow had popped into my head like that, I've no idea.

We were soon back at the hotel, so we said our goodnights and arranged to spend the next day on the beach together.

oOo

I MANAGED to have an hour or so to myself the next day, so I wandered into town to find a nice gift for Ryan. I was still unsure what to buy, so I finally settled on a gold necklace – I knew he would have to take it off for his martial arts lessons, but…basically, I didn't know what else to buy. While I was wandering around town, I also took my camera in to get some of the photos printed off. One was the perfect picture of Ryan and me, so I bought a frame for it. I would give that to him, too.

On Wednesday, we headed up the Monchique mountain, where we'd been advised to visit, particularly for chicken piri-piri. We had a lovely day up there, visiting local artisan shops and stopping for coffee at the very summit. On the way back down, we stopped for chicken, to see what all the fuss was about. It was grilled on the barbecue and basted with a special chilli sauce, and served with salad and chips, accompanied by a bottle of cheap red wine. Perfect.

We spent the evening in Praia da Rocha again, where we drank and danced until the early hours of the following morning.

Ryan and I were aware of how little time we had left together, and we tried not to let it get us down, but it was tough. Hugh had managed to get the same flight home as Gwen and I, and we were leaving on Saturday morning. Ryan and Brad were flying back to the States on Sunday via a stop in Lisbon. It was such an awful thought, so I kept trying to push it to the back of my mind, but occasionally it would spring back and smack me in the face.

Thursday we spent by the pool at the hotel with Brad, Hugh and Gwen, but we soon came to realise that we needed some time to ourselves, so Ryan had a word with Brad and explained. Of course, he understood and stayed with Gwen and Hugh while we headed off for a walk.

Ryan held my hand so tight it hurt. Eventually, I told him, and he apologised and laughed. 'I'm sorry, Summer. I just can't help thinking about Saturday without you.'

I put my finger to his lips and told him not to mention it. 'Ssshhh. Let's not talk about that. We have two days left. Let's make the most of them. We can buy some champagne and go to the hotel. I want you all to myself...I don't want to be surrounded by all these people. I just want it to be you and me. Okay?'

He nodded. Then we quickly bought some chilled champagne and went back to my room. He opened it, and I said that it was to celebrate the fantastic times we'd spent together.

We drank a few glasses and then slowly undressed, admiring each other.

'God, Summer, I never want this to end,' he said as he pulled me towards him and held me, our naked bodies intertwined as if we were one.

We lay on the bed and did nothing but kiss for hours until we could take it no more. We had to have each other.

He caressed me, and I caressed him. He kissed me all over, from head to toe, and I did the same to him. It was all so slow and sensuous.

When he entered me, I exploded. Then he exploded, too. And we repeated it over and over and over. The only word I could use to describe it was magical. Never before had I received and given so much pleasure. We showered together afterwards, and then we did it all again and again and again.

But before we knew it, it was Friday.

Neither Gwen nor Brad had interrupted us because they'd just known. They knew we needed that time together. It was the most exciting and miraculous time I'd had in my entire life. God, I was going to miss him, but, boy, what memories they would be. Memories I would cherish forever.

We spent all day Friday talking and repeating Thursday's performance. But not once did we speak about the future. He tried, but I wouldn't let him go on.

Then, in the evening, we knew we had to leave the room. It was my last night, so we had to go out with the rest of the group.

At seven, we were ready to join the others, but with a sad look in our eyes. We had all become such great friends over the past two weeks, and it was difficult to leave it all behind. It was hard to believe I had known this man and his best friend for only two weeks. I felt like I'd known them forever.

We wanted to really enjoy that last night together, so we went to the restaurant where we'd eaten on our first evening out together. We had the best night of the entire two weeks. Afterwards, we went to the bar down at the marina for a few drinks but soon headed back to the hotel. We couldn't stay up too late because of our journey back home the following morning.

Ryan was spending the night with me, so I had to say goodbye to Brad, and Gwen and Hugh to Ryan.

'Well, you guys, I guess this is it!' Brad said.

'Yep... God, I'm gonna really miss you, Brad,' sobbed Gwen as she gave him a huge hug.

'I wish you guys could come to the wedding.' Gwen had already asked them, but they'd said they couldn't because they weren't able to take another vacation so soon because of business. 'But perhaps we'll see you in August, on our honeymoon. We don't know if we're going to America yet, but...maybe,' she sobbed, wiping her eyes with her sleeve.

'Try to, it'll be great to see you both again, and for you to meet Cherry,' he said. 'You take care of that lil' baby in there, okay?'

Hugh shook hands with Brad and Ryan, and once again thanked them for looking after Gwen at the hospital. 'It's been great, it really has.'

And then Gwen turned to Ryan and hugged him. 'I'm going to

miss you, too. God, I hate goodbyes,' she sobbed, and she quickly rushed into the hotel.

Then it was my turn to say goodbye to Brad.

'Well, goodbye. You're great, you know that? Cherry is such a lucky girl. You be sure to tell her that, okay?' He nodded. 'And… and you look after Ryan for me, okay?' I guess he just knew what I was saying. I was telling him that I really wouldn't be seeing him or Ryan again.

He pulled me towards him and gave me a big hug, whispering, 'Don't make any rash decisions, Summer. Remember what I said about fate. I really believe that y'know? And I do think we'll be seeing you again. Until then, you take good care of yourself. Farewell, Summer. I'll miss ya. I sure will miss ya!'

His intentions were good, they really were, but I kept telling myself that he was wrong. There was no point in kidding myself that it would work. And that was that.

Brad waved as he headed back to his hotel, and Ryan and I went up to my room, where we spent hours making the most remarkable love…ever. It was even more intoxicating and astounding than earlier. Perhaps it was my way of saying goodbye.

At five in the morning, I knew I had to start getting ready to go. The coach was picking us up at six, so I climbed out of bed and looked at him. The most gorgeous guy. He opened his eyes and said, 'This is it, isn't it?' I nodded, unable to speak properly.

I managed to whisper, 'Will you shower with me first?'

He walked into the bathroom with me, and we climbed in together, where we made love one last time.

Just before six, I was all packed and dressed. I'd cried since the shower, so I wasn't looking too great. But before I walked down to the coach, I gave him his gifts but told him not to open them until I'd gone. I didn't want him to go to the coach with me. I couldn't bear that, and from the look on his face, neither could he.

He handed me his email address and contact details, but I told him I didn't want them. He didn't understand. I said it would never work, we couldn't continue a relationship living in two countries. He shook his head in disagreement. He was clearly distraught.

'B-but Summer…I lo—'

I stopped him from saying it. I couldn't listen to him saying it, and I couldn't tell him that I felt the same way. Shaking my head and trying to hold my head up high, I kissed him. One last kiss goodbye. 'It's over, Ryan. Goodbye.'

I tried to be cool and calm, but it was the most challenging thing I'd ever had to do. I picked up my suitcase and rushed out of the hotel, without a glance backwards. If I'd have looked, I'd have broken down. I couldn't. I just couldn't.

Gwen and Hugh were waiting on the coach for me. In fact, I was the only one the coach was waiting for. I slumped down next to them, and Gwen put her arms around me. Hugh patted my hand in understanding. I didn't look up out of the window. I knew Ryan was there.

Several hours later, when we were on the plane heading back to dreary old England, Gwen tried to get me to eat something.

'C'mon, Summer, just eat a little bit, you need to eat.'

I tried, but you know what plane food is like. Plus, I felt like shit. I'd just lost the most amazing man, and it was all because of me. He must have thought I was an absolute bitch. I told Gwen what I was thinking, and she shook her head.

'No, he doesn't think that at all. In fact, Ryan knew what you were going to do. I don't know how he knew, but he knew you were going to end it.'

She took something out of her handbag and handed it to me.

'He asked me to give this to you when we were on the plane.'

I opened the box to find the most exquisite necklace, with matching bracelet and earrings. Inside the box was a hand-written message:

Dearest Summer,

I understand.

I love you.

Ryan

I tried so hard not to cry; I sniffed the tears back but eventually howled. Everyone on the plane turned to see who the sniffling silly cow was. Well, it was me, and I didn't care what they all thought. They could all get stuffed. Big time.

CHAPTER 9

inally, I was home. Gwen asked if I wanted her to stay with me, but I said it was probably a good idea for me to be alone. I had to get over it myself. I needed to work things out in my head.

The first thing I noticed when I walked through the door was the answerphone; it was full of messages. I listened to them all. Every single one of them was from Grayson. In each one, he sounded more distressed and hurt than the last. I guess I felt sorry for him. I'd got to the stage where I didn't really care what he'd done to me a couple of weeks before. From the sound of those messages, he'd been in enough pain. Still, I wasn't going to phone him. If he wanted to explain, he'd have to call me. Mind you, did I really care? Not exactly. He had hurt me too.

It was early Saturday afternoon, and there was no food in the flat, so I figured I'd better pop out to get some. But first, I slogged up to Gwen's to see if she wanted anything. Hugh was picking her up to go round to his place, so she declined.

'Are you sure you're okay, Luv? You've been through a lot lately. Just so you know, I'm here if you need me, okay?'

I nodded gratefully. 'I'll be fine, Gwen. I've just had the best two weeks of my life. I know I didn't end it too well, but it's time I sorted my life out anyway. I'm not going to see Ryan again, but I've got some amazing memories. Now it's time for me to move on. But thanks for being here for me.'

She smiled at me. 'You know, it's strange, but you've changed a lot in the past couple of weeks. You seem to have grown up a lot. I'm thrilled that we're the best pals in the whole world.'

I gave her a big hug and headed downstairs, out the door and down to Sainsbury's. In the car on my way there, in the supermarket and all the way back, all I could think about was Ryan, and in particular, our final days together. The most amazing lovemaking ever to exist on this Earth. It had been wonderful. And now it was over. It was hard, but it had been my call, and ending it had been the only way I could move forward with my life. Ryan was a genuinely extraordinary guy, who deserved only the best; having a relationship with me in a different country wasn't that. He deserved better than me, and I'd seen to it that he could have that opportunity. But, boy was it hard.

I had a sudden flashback on that first day on the beach, when I'd lost my bikini top, and he'd found it for me. I smiled. I had some great memories that I would always cherish and hoped he would cherish them too.

I finally pulled up back outside my apartment, lucky to find a parking spot so close, and carried in my shopping. But waiting for me outside the door was Grayson.

He looked terrible. Tired and unshaven, and I wondered how he could manage to pull paying customers looking like that. The second he saw me, his eyes brightened, and he jumped up from where he'd been sitting by the doorstep.

I stopped, not quite sure what to say or do. I settled for a meagre, 'Hello, Grayson.'

'Hello, Grayson? That's all you're going to say after standing me up like that and buggering off for two weeks without even a single note?'

I thought the word 'buggering' was just a tad inappropriate.

Unlocking the door while juggling the carrier bags in my hands, he tried to help me, but I made it quite clear that the last thing I wanted from him was help.

'Summer, what the hell is going on?' He managed to push the

door open and grab a bag just before I let it slip from my fingers. 'Speak to me, Summer. Have I done something so bad that I deserve this kind of treatment?'

Suddenly I laughed, and he shrank away from me as if I was going to turn him into a frog or something. 'You don't know? You haven't figured it out yet?' I spat.

He shook his head. 'I really don't know what all this is about. I think you could at least explain. You owe me that much, Summer. And I'm not leaving until you've given me an explanation.' He sat down at the kitchen table, his arms crossed, staring at me as if I was pure evil.

'I owe you an explanation?' I shrieked. 'You? How dare you. How dare you!'

I was quite impressed with myself, actually. He was looking slightly terrified as if at any moment I might produce a cleaver and cut off his head.

'Summer, please,' he whimpered, like an animal.

'You son of a bitch. How dare you say that I owe you an explanation,' I seethed.

'Oh, for Christ's sake, I've obviously done something wrong. Something so wrong for you to hop on a plane and leave the country for a couple of weeks without even a note. Spit it out. What is it? What the hell have I done, which is so bad, Summer?' he shouted, his eyes reddening with tension before he calmed down and whispered, 'I thought we had something great starting. We were getting on so well.' His eyes searched mine for some of that affection he'd created just weeks previously.

Okay, so maybe I did owe him an explanation. This was going to be a long afternoon. My shoulders sagged as I filled the kettle. 'Coffee?' I mumbled.

He nodded, waiting for me to start to explain. After all, he had been waiting for two weeks. He never took his eyes off me while I poured the coffee and sat down in front of him, handing him his. Then, very slowly, I began.

'Okay, Grayson, you want to know what was so bad, then I'll tell you. I guess it started with the magazines.'

He looked questioningly at me.

'The women's magazines. You seemed to have a rather unhealthy obsession with them. I didn't think much of it, at first, but then, of course, was the make-up. You said it belonged to your sister. But you don't have a sister, do you, Grayson?'

He looked at me and slowly shook his head.

'I suspected you didn't have one when you couldn't even remember her name. A brother not knowing his sister's name. A bit odd, wouldn't you think?'

He tried to interrupt me.

'No, Grayson. You wanted an explanation, and that's what you're going to get. So don't interrupt me. Don't speak. Let me talk first, okay?'

Again he nodded silently and listened to what I had to say.

'We watched those videos, and all you could talk about was what the women were wearing. You sounded like a woman, for God's sake. I thought how strange it was, but then I made excuses for you because I guess I was beginning to fall for you. I even had an argument with Gwen over you. She saw the strange reality. I didn't. I couldn't. And then, one night I went to see my mum, and on the way back I decided to go and see you. Only I was in for quite a surprise. Leaving your flat was a tall blond person, wearing a great deal of make-up, a tight pink dress and very high pink stilettos that this person couldn't really walk very well in. At first, I thought it was your sister, so I called out the name you'd given me. Emily, I think it was. But nothing happened. I followed her. I'm sure you can imagine my surprise when she stopped at the Red Light District. I was in shock, I figured you'd been sleeping with a hooker.'

He shook his head, tears welling up in his eyes. I shook my head at him and told him not to say a word.

'I walked home in a daze. It was awful. The man I was falling for was sleeping with someone else, but not just anybody else. A prostitute, for God's sake. What did that say for me? Was I that awful? I cried my eyes out and went straight up to see Gwen. I stayed with her that night and the next day, I even went to a...' I stopped and cringed, 'I even went to a doctor...to make sure I hadn't contracted any kind of disease or anything.'

'God, Summer...' he muttered.

I shook my head at him again. 'No, Grayson. I haven't finished. Soon afterwards, Gwen and I began to put two and two together. We'd watched a talk show about transvestites. You fitted the bill perfectly. And I'd even noticed that the so-called 'woman' that left your flat actually looked a lot like you. Can you imagine how dirty and disgusting that made me feel?'

I finally stopped, tears slowly pouring down my face. I hated him then. He tried to take my hand, but I pulled it away quickly, not wanting to be touched by him.

'Summer, Summer, Summer,' he whispered. 'You've got it all wrong. That wasn't me. I swear to you. It wasn't. I realise that's really hard to believe, right now. All the signs pointed to me like that. But it's not like that at all. Please believe me,' he said pleadingly.

'It wasn't you, but you were sleeping with a hooker, is that it?'

He hesitated.

I shook my head. 'You can't even tell me the truth now, can you? Well, Grayson Rosenblum, if you won't tell me the truth, I want nothing to do with you...ever. Do you understand? I want you out of my house now.' I began shaking uncontrollably with anger. He wanted me to believe him, but he wouldn't tell me the goddamn truth.

'No,' he uttered under his breath, 'I'm not going anywhere. I don't want it to end like this, Summer. Can't you see? Can't you see that... I' m-I'm, oh shit. Summer, I'm in love with you.'

Bloody hell! He had a peculiar way of showing it.

'Jesus, Grayson. You don't know the meaning of love. If you love someone you sure as hell don't sleep with hookers and lie to them.' God, if Gwen were here she'd be laughing, I thought. In fact, if I were in a different frame of mind, I'd be laughing. 'Look, if you loved me like you say you do ...you'd come clean. You'd tell me the truth,' I whispered, softening a little.

It was almost five o'clock by then.

'Shit, I think I need a drink. Do you have anything stronger?' he asked.

I stood up and opened the drinks cupboard. 'Brandy?'

He nodded. I poured two, and we went and sat in the living room.

'Okay, Summer. To prove that I have fallen in love with you, I'll tell you the truth. And I have never, ever, told a soul about this.' His eyes began to well up with tears once again as he slowly explained. 'I don't have a sister. I don't have brothers either. In fact, I don't even have a father. The woman you saw, leaving my flat... was—was... my m-mother.'

I gasped. Shit, his mum was a prostitute. Incest?

'She is a prostitute. She has been since she was thirteen years old. She was orphaned as a child, and she couldn't handle the orphanage, so she ran away and lived on the streets.' He took a massive gulp of brandy and continued. 'At fourteen she became pregnant by a "client", and I was the result.'

I felt terrible.

'All she has ever known is prostitution. Even just after I was born, she went straight back to it. She shared a tiny flat with a few other girls who were all in the same business. They took it in turns to look after me. I thought it was normal as I was growing up. I figured most mums did it, but when I went to school, I saw that my mum wasn't like other mums. I became ashamed and embarrassed. It was humiliating. Occasionally she would go to parents' evening, dressed ready to go out with her tight tiny clothes and high heels with lots of make-up. It didn't take long for people to realise my mum was working on the streets. Lots of kids weren't allowed to be my friend, in case they caught something. Some parents were even afraid my mum would take their pocket money in exchange for sex!' He smiled faintly. 'She would never do anything to harm any of those kids. She only sold herself to consenting adults.'

I was so shocked. No wonder he'd wanted to keep this from me. He was so ashamed of his past that he didn't want anyone to know about it. I felt truly and utterly awful for him. Especially for the accusations I'd made. He needed someone. Badly. And I'd assumed the worst.

'And she still does it now?' I whispered.

'Yeah. She's forty-five years old and is still a prostitute. She couldn't do anything else. She wouldn't know how.'

'So the magazines and make-up? Your mum's?'

He nodded. 'Uh, huh. I buy them for her in the hope that she'll read about prostitution and see that it's no proper way to live, and maybe…she might be given other ideas. Sometimes, if her flat-mates have clients at their place and she needs to freshen up and stuff, she drops by my flat. I've told her to make sure no-one sees her.'

'Does she know that you're ashamed of what she does?'

'Of course. But it doesn't make any difference. I've even offered for her to come and live with me and I'll support her. But it's no use. It's what she wants to do, and I can't stop her. She's been in jail a few times, too. But…it makes no difference.'

He'd poured his heart out to me. I was grateful for that, and I respected him for doing it.

'Grayson? I hope you can forgive me,' I asked as I got up and sat down beside him, holding his hand.

He nodded again and apologised for not telling me before. 'I realise that it's a lot to take in. I really wish I'd have told you before.'

But if he had, I'd never have met Ryan.

'Can we start afresh?'

I wasn't sure that was such a great idea, considering I was getting over the love of my life. But I figured Grayson deserved another chance. I mean, I'd almost fallen for him some weeks ago, but it had all got screwed up. I needed time. I had to think things through, and I told him that. But I didn't tell him about Ryan. That wasn't fair on him.

'I understand,' he said.

Those two words suddenly wrenched at my heart. I under-stand; that's what Ryan had written on the jewellery box.

'Are you alright, Summer? You look like you're in pain.'

I shook my head with a sad smile. 'No, I'm fine, really, I am.'

We stood up at the same time, and Grayson held me tight. 'Gosh, I've waited two whole weeks to feel like this again, Summer,' he said, as he gently stroked the top of my head. But I was miles away…in Portugal, with Ryan.

I pushed the thought back to the dark recesses of my mind and came back to reality. 'Grayson?'

'Uh, huh?'

'Will you give me some time to think things through?'

'Of course. Just don't go running off for another couple of weeks without a word, okay?'

I nodded with a smile. He gently kissed my cheek and walked backwards out of the room. 'I'll wait for you. As long as it takes. I'll be here for you.' And then he was gone.

CHAPTER 10

July had been a tough month. Not only was I desperately trying to get over Portugal, but I was also trying to come to terms with Grayson's dark past. I'd thought about Ryan almost every second of every day and often cried myself to sleep. But I knew I had to sort myself out, so I'd called Grayson and told him I was willing to give it another shot. I wasn't prepared to sleep with him just yet, though. I explained that sex shouldn't be something taken lightly. I wanted to respect him for who he was, and I wanted him to do the same. I wasn't interested in him for whether or not he was good in bed, I wanted to learn to love him for what was inside him, in his head and in his heart.

He was ecstatic. Over the moon. And considering his past with his mum, he totally agreed with my decision about not sleeping together. The day after I'd phoned him, I'd arrived at work to find a huge bouquet of roses on my desk. Initially, my heart had almost jumped out of my mouth—had Ryan found me? But when I read the note, I discovered they were from Grayson.

Beautiful roses for a beautiful girl.

Thank you for giving me another chance.

Love Grayson.

My colleagues had been suitably impressed. Ricki almost

collapsed with envy. 'Wow, you lucky girl. I wish someone would send me flowers.'

'Somebody will, someday soon, I'm sure of it.' I smiled.

It was strange, but since my return from Portugal, Ricki and I had actually become friends, and even Gavin and Geoff seemed different; friendlier towards me. I don't know. Gwen said that she'd seen a difference in me. Said I'd grown up a lot. Maybe I had. I could perhaps thank Ryan for that.

oOo

IT WAS FINALLY AUGUST. In just a few more weeks, Gwen and Hugh would be tying the knot. I was almost as excited as she was as we headed into town to try on her wedding gown and my brides-maid's dress.

'I can't believe how big your tummy has grown,' I said, tenderly patting her bump.

She chuckled, putting her hand on her lower back as she stretched. 'Yeah, I know. It doesn't half give me backache, though.'

'Do you want to stop and sit down for a minute?'

'Why don't we stop at a coffee shop or something and have a drink and a bite to eat?'

'Sounds good to me.'

We stopped at the nearest one, enjoying tea and muffins before setting off for the bridal shop again.

'So how are things with you and Grayson, then?'

'Not bad, actually.' I smiled.

'But?' She knew me so well; she always knew when something wasn't quite right.

'But …he's not Ryan.'

'I knew that's what you were going to say. But you made your choice. You decided to give Ryan up in Portugal. You said yourself that it was the right thing to do. You couldn't continue a relation-ship with someone that lived halfway across the world. And now you've got Grayson. Who, after coming completely clean, has turned out to be a lovely guy. You should be happy with him. Did you tell him the nickname we gave him?'

I laughed. 'God, no!'

I'd confided in Gwen and told her all about Grayson's past. He'd said it was okay. He knew I had to tell her because she'd come to the same conclusion I had. And if we were all going to be friends, he didn't want to have any secrets. It was a sweet way of thinking, I suppose.

'Are you happy with him?'

I stopped and thought about it for a few seconds. 'Yeah, I guess so. Although sometimes I see him more as a pal than a boyfriend. Actually, I kind of see him that way all the time. But I don't want to hurt him. And maybe someday I'll begin to love him the way he deserves to be loved.'

Gwen shook her head, the edges of her mouth turning upwards slightly.

'What?'

'Nothing. It's nothing.'

Before I had the chance to grill her some more, we were at the bridal shop, and Gwen had walked inside.

'Miss Pursehouse. How lovely to see you. I see your bump has grown a little since we last saw you,' said a very gay young man who bounded towards us like a giant puppy dog.

'Hello, George,' Gwen replied happily, slumping down in a chair while he fetched her dress.

'Here we go. As you can see, I've elasticated the waistband underneath, so it will be more comfortable for you. Would you like me to assist you?'

'Actually, I'd prefer Gwen to give me a hand, if that's okay?' she said, looking just a little uncomfortable.

'Of course.'

I took the dress for her as she stood up and headed for the dressing room, where I hung it up and helped her out of her clothes.

A whole twenty minutes later, we walked out of the dressing room and stood in front of the mirror.

Gwen looked astoundingly beautiful, like a fairytale princess. I told her so, and she said that was precisely how she felt. She did a little twirl (to the best of her ability, considering her bulging tummy) and George exclaimed, 'My, oh my. Miss Pursehouse, you look positively radiant. Stunning. Stunning,' while clasping his hands close to his chest.

'Oh, George. I've told you a thousand times, call me Gwen, will you?'

He blushed and said, 'Oh, alright...Gwen.' He was obviously quite taken with her.

'George, it's beautiful. Really, really beautiful,' I said quietly and congratulated him on the design and the exquisite detail he'd put into it.

It was an extraordinary dress. Ivory in colour, with lace and pearls sewn into the bodice, it flared out at the back into a relatively long train. The front was long and simple, but it seemed to hide Gwen's protruding pregnant belly. It had no sleeves – Gwen was lucky to be able to go sleeveless as her boobs were big enough to fill the top of the dress but not too big to overpower the look, and her arms were slim and toned.

Not only had George designed and made Gwen's wedding dress to suit her perfectly, but he'd also designed and made my bridesmaid dress, which was pale pink. It was similar to hers, except mine had shoestring straps (unfortunately for me, I didn't have the boobs to hold it up) and didn't have a long train at the back. Also, I'd asked George not to include pearls on mine—I didn't want my dress to be as impressive as hers. It was her wedding, so it was only right that her dress should have all the details. Mine should just be simple, and he understood perfectly. When I tried it on, it was almost perfect. There was just something missing. I stood in front of the mirror, turning from one side to the other. What was it? And then I knew. The necklace, bracelet and ear-rings Ryan had bought for me. They'd go perfectly with it. I put my hand up to my neck and imagined.

Gwen saw me smile and nodded in acknowledgement. 'You're right, y' know.'

'About what? What do you mean?'

'The jewellery from Ryan. It will look stunning with the dress.'

'How did you know that's what I was thinking?'

She winked at me and chuckled. 'You forget, Luv, I know you better than you know yourself. You look gorgeous. If only Ryan could see you now.'

I sighed and headed back to the dressing room.

George followed. 'How do you like it, Miss Miller?'

I smiled, told him my name was Summer and said I loved it. 'You've done the most perfect job with both our dresses, George. Thank you so much.' I gave him a little peck on the cheek, and he reddened and clapped his hands in delight.

After we'd changed back into our everyday clothes, we told George we'd be back a couple of days before the wedding to pick up the dresses and to make sure we hadn't ballooned or suddenly slimmed down or anything. He laughed, and we were just about to step out of the shop when Gwen exclaimed, 'George, I nearly forgot!'

She rummaged through her handbag until she found what she was looking for. She handed him a beautiful white and gold envelope.

'It's an invitation to the wedding. I'd really like it if you could come. And please, bring your partner.'

George almost jumped up and down with excitement. 'Oh, Miss Pur—I mean, Gwen. Thank you so much. Of course, we'll be delighted to attend. It's so exciting. Thank you so much!' Clearly thrilled, he leaned forward and pecked her on the cheek, before we headed out of the shop. All of us grinned from ear to ear.

'You certainly made George's day.'

'He's such a sweet man that Hugh and I thought it would be great for him and his partner to come too.'

'You're so sweet, Gwen.'

She laughed and said she knew she was, as we headed to the hairdressing salon. Gwen had her headdress with her, and I had a lovely little tiara. We were just going to show them to the hairdresser, to give her an idea of what she was going to work with.

She was called Alison, and Gwen had also invited her to the wedding; she'd been doing our hair for the past few years, so we knew her well. Alison was our age and very popular with many people in their twenties in the area. As well as being able to do simple cuts and styles, she was also excellent at more dramatic cuts and colours. In fact, her own hair was very long and simple but had a multitude of different colours intertwined in it like a rainbow. She was a pretty girl who'd got married the year before, to a plumber called Steve. They were the perfect couple—almost like Gwen and Hugh, or...Ryan and me.

We gave her free rein with our hair. She was the expert; it was up to her to decide what to do with it. That was the way she preferred it.

Working alongside her was another friend of ours, Billy, who was only nineteen but was a beautician magician—a pro with all things relating to make-up. She could probably make the Queen look like Britney Spears. So I was thrilled for my face to be left in her capable hands on the wedding day.

After an hour or so of experiments, Gwen and I came out feeling totally confident that we were going to look like princesses on August 25th.

'So is everything finalised for the day, then?' I asked as we drove back home.

'Yup. Obviously, the church and reception have been booked, because the invitations have already been sent out, and we managed to find a great group who do Motown, disco, pop, the works. I can't wait.'

'What are they called? The group that is.'

'Erm, it's a weird name. Hang on, I think I've got their card in my wallet,' she said as she tried to find it. 'Here it is. Musicantasy. Different, I suppose. But they're good. Oh, I forgot to tell you. Hugh has booked the honeymoon. We're off to America.'

'Wow, you lucky thing,' I yelled, but all I could think of was Ryan. She knew what was going through my mind, but she didn't say anything. In fact, she didn't bother mentioning the honeymoon again after that. I guess she didn't want to upset me.

We managed to park the car outside our flats. Gwen was still living there. She'd told Hugh she would move in with him after the wedding, which meant she still had a month of independence. He'd been a bit concerned at first, what with the baby and stuff, but she said I only lived downstairs, so if there was ever anything wrong, I was there if she needed me. He seemed okay with that, although he did bring it up in conversation every now and again. We simply told him to shut up and stop moaning.

I walked up to her flat with her—one of the things Hugh had asked me to do whenever possible. 'You will make sure she gets up those stairs okay, if you're around, won't you?'

'Of course, Hugh, three bags full, Hugh,' I'd said.

He was funny. Such a worrier.

Once back at home, I got out the photo album and sat down.

It was something I did often; I just sat and flicked through all the photos from Portugal. Ryan and me at the water park. Ryan and me in Monchique, eating piri piri chicken, Ryan and me chasing each other around the beach at the west coast, Ryan and me eating steak with bibs on. Ryan and me lazing by the pool drinking cocktails. Ryan and me boogying away in a night club. Ryan and I on the cliff tops in Praia do Carvoeiro. I cried every time I looked at them. They brought back so many wonderful memories. The album stayed under my bed because I didn't want Grayson to see it. I still hadn't told him about my holiday fling. He'd noticed I'd changed a lot since then, but I think he blamed himself. I know it was cruel of me to let him go on thinking that, but it would be really cruel if he found out after all this time that I'd fallen in love with someone else on that trip.

There was a sudden knock on the door that scared the shit out of me. 'Who is it?'

'It's me – I brought food.' Grayson's voice was muffled by the door.

'Er, hang on a minute, Grayson,' I shouted as I scuttled into the bedroom and pushed the album back underneath the bed. Quickly peering in the mirror, I noticed my eyes were red. Shit. I looked like I'd been crying, so I ran into the kitchen and grabbed an onion, quickly slicing it in half. God, I'm good, I thought. 'I'm coming. Just a sec!'

'Hello, gorgeous! Oh, you've been crying. What's wrong?' he said as I opened the door.

'No, I haven't. Chopping an onion, see?' I said as I held the onion and knife in one hand.

He kissed me gently, almost on the lips. I moved, so it landed on my cheek.

'Don't you usually peel onions before chopping them?'

'I was just going to use half. I was about to make dinner, I wasn't expecting you.'

'I hope you haven't got very far with it because I brought Chinese takeaway.' He grinned, holding up the bag, which smelled divine.

'Erm, no, all I did was chop an onion,' I said as I tossed it into the bin. 'What's the occasion?'

'Does there have to be an occasion to bring my girlfriend food?'

I smiled. 'Of course not. What do you want to drink?'

'Wine would be great.'

'Oh, I'm afraid I don't have any,' I said, but he quickly produced a bottle from his carrier bag with a grin.

'That's why I brought a bottle with me.'

'Smart thinking, Batman,' I laughed, nudging him with my shoulder.

We took out the food, poured the wine and sat on the couch with the TV on while we ate a delicious combination of prawn crackers, chicken with almonds, spring rolls, pork chap soi and spare ribs. Finger-lickin' good.

'So how's your mum? Have you seen her lately?' I asked as I sucked the sauce off one of the ribs.

'I saw her yesterday, actually. She's not too bad. Same as always, I guess.'

'Am I ever going to meet her?'

'You mean you want to? After what I told you about her?'

'Why not?'

He smiled. 'She'd be thrilled to meet you, I'm sure. Considering I've never let her meet any of my friends.'

'It's a date, then.'

'Cool.'

Curious, I asked him if she were the reason he'd split with his previous girlfriend, but he explained that she'd dumped him because he was always so busy with work commitments and other things. 'She didn't know about my mum. You're the first person I've told.'

I nodded, smiled and turned my attention back to the TV, taking a long swig of wine.

I felt Grayson's hands on my shoulders, he slowly began to rub them, and suddenly I had a flashback to Portugal. Ryan and I were at the waterpark, and he was massaging my back. Absolute ecstasy.

'What did you say?'

'Huh?' I was brought right back to the present day.

'Didn't you say something? It sounded like "Ryan" or something?'

'No, you must have been hearing things. Maybe it was the TV.' Shit, that was close. But what a wonderful thought.

'Summer?'

'Mmm?'

'Erm... I was just wondering if... if... you were ready...for y' know?'

'Erm, actually I don't know. What are you on about?' I asked.

He told me in plain terms that he was wondering if I was ready for a sexual relationship with him yet. It had been over a month.

I understood he was probably feeling frustrated, but I wasn't ready. The problem was, maybe I'd never be ready to have sex with him. Maybe I'd never be ready to have sex with anyone other than Ryan. Maybe I should just give up now and become a nun. 'I'm sorry, Grayson. But it's still too soon. No, I'm not ready yet. Please just give me a bit more time.'

I could see him beginning to get a bit tense and irritated. 'Is there something wrong with me?'

'Of course not.'

'But you won't even kiss me the way you used to. If I go to kiss you on the lips, you move your head to the side. It doesn't make me feel too good, you know.'

'I'm sorry,' I said, moving closer to him. 'There really is nothing wrong with you. It's me. Not you.' To prove it, I put my arms around him. I had to kiss him some time. You never know, maybe there would be fireworks like there was with Ryan. I leaned forward and kissed him hard on the lips. Our tongues met in the middle. It was a bit messy and no... No fireworks. No fire. Not even a spark. Well, perhaps I should give it time.

He pulled away from me and smiled. 'That's more like it,' he said.

Inside I cringed.

CHAPTER 11

It was Thursday, August 23rd. Gwen and I had picked up our dresses from George's bridal shop and were back at home getting ready for the hen party that night.

'I can't believe you invited George,' I gasped.

'It'll be hilarious. George is definitely the 'female' one in that couple, so he'll be just like one of the girls,' she giggled.

We were going to a strip club with a difference. It had a restaurant where the waiters were virtually naked, and all the strippers were male. It was going to be an absolute blast.

Gwen decided to wear the little denim dress that I'd bought for her in Portugal, and I wore a sexy short pink dress with pink and brown sandals and a small brown handbag.

The others were coming round to my flat at seven for a few drinks, and then we were being picked up by a limo at 8.30.

Alison, Billy, George and Ricki all arrived on time. As soon as they came into my flat, where Gwen and I were already waiting for them, I'd taken out the camera and began taking pictures of everyone. Gwen was showered with gifts, which included a hilarious battery-powered giant tongue, a huge, rudely phallic-shaped teddy, a bottle of liquor shaped like a penis and the Kama Sutra.

'She won't need any of these things, because she's already pregnant,' I announced.

'Well, can I borrow them then?' piped George, who was clearly getting into the swing of things.

We all fell about laughing as we made jokes, drank plenty of cocktails (Gwen's were non-alcoholic) and generally had a great time.

The limo arrived right on time, and I managed to convince the driver to take a few photos of the group, which he did. In fact he got a bit carried away, so much so that I was worried the camera would run out of memory!

In the limo, we had a glass of champagne and sang old songs, like Samantha Fox's Touch Me and Madonna's Like a Virgin. It was great. We arrived at the club for nine and were shown to our table by a Robbie Williams look-a-like who wore nothing but a leather thong. I popped a tip into his 'pouch' and pinched his bum as the rest of the group nearly fell off their seats, laughing at my brazen cheekiness.

Choosing something from the menu was particularly tricky with all those sexy bodies and bums parading around the table all the time. Poor George was a bit of mess. This was probably something he'd always dreamed of but never thought he'd get the chance to see. I splashed his face with cold water every now and again, to try and calm him down, and Gwen giggled constantly.

After dinner, we were shown into another room full of women; the music was loud and pumping, and dry ice wafted throughout. Up on stage, in various locations throughout the room, were big muscly men, stripping off or rubbing baby oil onto themselves. The atmosphere was nothing less than fantastic. Women danced, watching hunks strut their stuff, and occasionally a stripper would bend down and ask to be joined by one of the women in the crowd.

I'd do anything for a laugh, so the next time one of them wanted to be joined by a woman, I made it quite clear I wanted to be picked.

It didn't take long for me to be hauled on stage by a real looker, even though he was probably gay. But I didn't care. He handed me a bottle of oil and told me to rub it in. I poured some on his huge chest and began rubbing sensuously, looking down to see where

Gwen and the others were. George looked up in pure envy and Alison, Billy and Ricki shrieked. Gwen was trying hard not to fall over from laughing so hard. Speaking of hard, maybe this guy wasn't gay after all! Either that or he had great control of his credentials, making it dance up and down.

I stopped rubbing in the oil, and he began gyrating against me. Yup, he was definitely a little on the hard side. My God—these guys got paid to do this all night long. What a job.

I had to admit, I was beginning to get all hot and flustered, a feeling I hadn't felt since Ryan. Finally, the stripper spoke and, guess what? He was American. That accent—yeah, It was nothing like Ryan's awesome Texan accent, but just listening to an American again... It was amazing. I could listen to him all night long. Mind you, I suppose I could gyrate with him all night long, too. Calm down, Summer, calm down.

'What's your name?' he whispered into my ear.

'Summer. What's yours?'

He gyrated some more, turned around to rub his tight bum against me as he played to the crowd. I laughed, and he turned back around.

'I'm Scott. It's been a pleasure dancing with ya, Summer. Maybe I'll see y' again, sometime?' He smiled, and I nodded and carefully placed a tip in his little leather pouch as I was helped back down by a couple of drool-worthy waiters.

'You lucky sod,' wailed Billy. I smiled and told her I'm sure she could get up there if she really wanted to, but she was clearly too embarrassed to even attempt it.

The rest of the evening went by so quickly, and before we knew it, it was 02h00. We would have liked to stay longer, but some of us had work the following day, and it wouldn't be good for the baby if Gwen didn't get home to bed too.

By 03h00, I was tucked up in bed, thinking of the usual things before I nodded off to sleep... Ryan. Mmm.

oOo

THE DAY of the wedding crept upon us. I awoke at seven, had a lovely relaxing shower, threw on my new tracksuit and ran upstairs, taking the steps two at a time, banging on Gwen's door.

'This is your wake-up call. Rise and shine, sleepy head. Blushing bride!'

The door opened and in I went, only to find an extremely nervous Gwen.

'You look petrified,' I laughed. 'This is going to be the best day of your life. You've got absolutely nothing to worry about or be nervous about. You are about to marry the loveliest man alive. So get with it, girl. Come on!'

Unusually for me, I was wide-awake. Pure excitement, I guess. Adrenaline was pumping for Gwen and for me. I'd never been a bridesmaid before, and Gwen sure as hell had never been a bride. I jogged past her into her kitchen and put the kettle on, making coffee for us both. We sat in the living room to drink it, and we chatted about the wedding and the hen night. She still avoided the subject of the honeymoon though, which was fine by me, because I preferred not to be reminded of Ryan in company if I could help it.

But today was her day, so I told her to talk about anything, even America.

'Actually, I forgot to tell you that stripper the other night was American. I could have listened to his voice all night long.'

'You mean you could have shagged him all night long!'

'No! But I could have gyrated fully clothed all night,' I laughed.

'Have you still not ... y' know... since Ryan?'

I sighed. 'No. It doesn't feel right.'

'It's been about two months, now. Don't you think it's about time you sorted yourself out? Poor Grayson must be banging it against the wall, by now.'

I chuckled but said nothing, preferring to change the subject. 'Do you want anything to eat?' I asked.

She shook her head. 'I'll probably throw up everywhere.'

'Charming. But you're gonna have to eat something. You won't be eating until the reception, which won't be until about three this afternoon. The last thing you want is your stomach rumbling throughout the church ceremony, do you?'

'I suppose you're right,' she mumbled.

'You go and get in the bath, or shower, or whatever it is you're doing, and I'll have a nice brekkie ready for you out here when you've finished. Okay?'

She grinned and nodded. 'What would I do without you, eh?'

'As you often say to me, that's something you'll never know because I'll always be here for you. You got that, soon-to-be Mrs Gwen Johnson?'

I ran back down to my flat and picked up the food I'd bought specially for breakfast: champagne, croissants, mild French cheese and smoked ham. I also decided to give her my special gift, the exquisite gold and white baby blanket. I took everything back upstairs and set the table. I put on some music—Vivaldi's Four Seasons. Extremely appropriate for a wedding morning, I thought.

Gwen came out of the shower, wearing a big white towelling robe and when she saw the table she looked at me with surprise, 'You really spoil me, you know?'

I nodded smugly. 'Before we eat, I want you to open this,' I said, handing her the parcel.

'What on Earth is this?'

'It's nothing for the wedding, but I figured it was a good time for you to open it.'

'Oh, my goodness. Wow. This is the most beautiful blanket I've ever laid eyes on. It's... It's exquisite. Thank you. Thank you so much.'

I noticed a couple of tears fall down her cheek as she jumped up to give me a big bear hug before we sat back down again.

'It's absolutely exquisite. Where did you buy it?'

'Portugal. I knew you'd love it.'

'I do… and so will Hugh.'

Alison and Billy arrived soon afterwards, bringing a change of clothes with them so they could get ready after they'd worked their magic on us. Alison's husband, Steve, was picking them up at midday to drive to the church.

We clinked champagne glasses and had a few sips before we

started to get ready for the big day. A few hours later, Gwen was all set. She looked positively radiant. In fact, when I first saw her, I cried; she was so beautiful. She said the same thing about me too, as Billy kindly took photos of the two us.

Then there was a knock at the door. Some of the guests were meeting at Gwen's place first, and of the first to arrive were her grandparents. Her granddad had happily agreed to give her away. In fact, he'd been so thrilled to be asked that he'd broken down and cried.

I opened the door for them. 'Grandma! Granddad!' They had always insisted I called them that, considering I was like a sister to Gwen.

'Summer, sweetie, yer lookin' great, kiddo,' Granddad said with a bear hug.

'Hello, Summer, dear. You do look beautiful.'

'Thank you. And so do you both. Was the hotel alright?' I asked as they walked into the lounge and Alison kindly poured them a glass of champagne each.

'Owtel were great stuff, kiddo. Ta fer bookin' it,' Grandad said with a grin.

I nodded, assuming he was thanking me for booking the hotel, just as Gwen walked in.

The looks on their faces were of pure pride. It brought tears to my eyes, which I tried to hold back, not wanting to mess up my immaculately done face. I was glad Billy had used waterproof mascara!

'Hello. Grandma… Granddad,' Gwen said shyly as she carefully hugged them.

'Oh, dear, a think am gonna cry,' sniffed Grandma. 'If only yer mum and dad could see yer now. A tell yer,' she sniffed, 'thed be so proud on yer.'

'Aye, they would. Yer look like a princess, luv.'

We all smiled and tried so hard not to cry. This was going to be one seriously emotional day.

More people began to arrive, and everyone commented on how gorgeous the bride and bridesmaid looked. We were in our element. Finally, Grayson turned up. He looked very handsome, in his posh suit, and he seemed to be speechless when he saw me. 'Wow! Summer. You look…gorgeous.'

'Why thank you, kind sir.'

When we were all set, everybody began heading to the church. Grayson kissed me on the cheek and said he'd see me there. Grandma was going with him. I was going in the Rolls with Gwen and Granddad.

We took our time, because the ceremony wasn't due to start for a little while, and it was the bride's prerogative to be a tad late. But Gwen didn't want to keep everyone waiting too long.

Her entrance at the church caused quite a stir. Naturally, there were gasps and whispers and the odd sniffle from the women. It was like something from a movie. Hugh was in total awe when he saw how beautiful his very soon-to-be wife looked.

The ceremony couldn't have been more perfect. Hugh didn't mess up his lines once, and the only hiccup was when the vicar asked if Gwen pledged to love and honour Huge Johnson instead of Hugh. I don't think everyone noticed, but I certainly did. So much so, in fact, that I tried not to laugh and ended up snorting, which caused some serious sniggers from the bride's side of the church. I felt guilty but noticed Gwen and Hugh had found it quite funny too, so I figured they'd probably forgive me. Oops!

The reception began wonderfully, and everybody was having a great time. There were about 150 guests there; more from Hugh's side than Gwen's though, but I knew a few of them. Ricki was there, and unfortunately, she didn't have a date, so she was looking pretty lonely.

'Hi, Ricki. Are you enjoying yourself?'

'Yeah, it's great,' she chirped, not wanting me to think she was actually feeling really sorry for herself.

'There are plenty of single men here, why don't you go and grab yourself one and show him your stuff on the dance floor?'

'I'm a bit shy, really,' she said, looking down towards her feet.

'I hear the best man's quite a catch.'

'Yeah?' she asked, suddenly quite keen to hear more.

'Uh, huh,' I nodded. 'He's over…' I looked around, trying to find him. 'There. See?'

She stood on tiptoes, even though she was wearing ridiculously high heels, and tried to focus on Neil, the best man.

Actually, I hadn't really heard he was a good catch, but he seemed like quite a nice bloke, and he wasn't ugly or anything. Mind you, he wasn't exactly Jake Gyllenhaal, either. But he was single.

'Why don't I introduce you to him?'

'That would be nice.' She smiled.

We walked over, and I tried to pair them off before I went for a walk, alone, around the grounds. Finding a little garden seat away from the entertainment, I sat down and looked up at the sky.

After all the emotion of seeing Gwen and Hugh tying the knot, I realised what I was doing to Grayson was cruel. I was leading him on. Leading him on the road to nowhere. It wasn't fair at all. I'd become a total bitch, and I didn't like it. I had to put a stop to it. Yep, that's what I would do. I had to tell him about my relationship with Ryan and the fact that I need to be alone to get over it. It was no good bringing him down with me. It wasn't fair. So I stood up, ready to go and look for Grayson, but as I turned around, he was standing right there behind me.

'Huh! Jesus! You scared the living daylights out of me.'

'Sorry, sweetheart.'

I cringed, suddenly realising that he wasn't going to take this very well at all.

'You look like you're on a mission or something,' he said.

Right, Summer... cut to the chase. Do it now. 'Grayson. I really need to talk to you. It's really important. I think we'd better sit down.'

We turned back to the wrought iron bench.

'What is it, Summer?' he said, concern written in the worried lines cutting into his forehead.

'I haven't been totally truthful with you lately, and I think it's about time I came clean. It's so unfair on you. Look...what I'm trying to say is that... Shit. Okay, right... I met someone when I was in Portugal.'

'Oh shit. You've been seeing someone else?'

'No... Yes. No. Well, the truth is that I fell in love with him, but I can't be with him.'

'What are you going on about, Summer? You're not making a great deal of sense here,' he said, standing up and pacing back and forth.

'Grayson, please sit down and listen to what I have to say. Please. Look, I met this great guy. We clicked, but he lives in America. So I ended it. There was no way we could carry on a relationship when we both live at opposite ends of the Earth.'

'So why are you telling me this?'

'Because I respect you, and I think you deserve to be treated a lot better than the way I've been treating you lately.'

He sat down. 'So why didn't you try treating me better and make an effort before?'

'I couldn't, Grayson. Don't you see that? I'm still in love with Ryan, and to be able to get over him, I need to be alone. I can't jump from one painful relationship to another like that. It wouldn't work between us. I need time. Maybe a great deal of time. Who knows, maybe too much time. Maybe I should become a nun or something.'

Grayson seemed to understand a lot better than I thought he would. Maybe he could see my pain. 'I wish you'd have told me about this when you returned from your holiday. I came clean with you, why didn't you come clean with me?'

'I didn't want to hurt you again, and I guess I didn't want to lose you once you told me about your past. You've become a great friend to me, and I really do hope that you can find it in your heart to forgive me for leading you on like this.'

He took my hand. 'These past few months have been tough for me because I've seen a distance and a pain in your eyes. I wanted you to tell me why, but I figured you would when the time was right.'

'Don't you hate me?'

'Of course I don't hate you. I guess you're becoming like the sister I never had. I know that sounds funny, but this business with the sex thing, I guess it's making me come to love and respect you differently too. Maybe I should call you Emily,' he joked.

I smiled, hugging him. 'Thank you, Grayson. I'm so sorry for giving you the run-around. I've been such a bitch.'

He kissed me on the cheek and hugged me. 'I get it; honestly, I do. I hate that you couldn't be honest with me, but I understand. I don't want to lose you, either. Now, if you don't object to dancing with your "brother", I quite fancy a boogie—or a slow dance. Whatever music comes next.'

Grayson held out his arm, which I held onto, and we walked back to the reception.

Needless to say, it was a slow dance. We laughed and chuckled as we stepped on each other's toes until the song ended. That's when I noticed Ricki standing alone at the side of the dance floor.

'Erm, Grayson, I hope you don't think this is a bit soon, but there's a lovely little lady over there who's dying for a dance,' I said as I winked at her.

He smiled and headed towards her while I walked away from the dance floor, watching as he led her to the floor just as a romantic song began.

What a great couple they made. Funny really. The very first day I'd noticed him, he'd been checking Ricki out. Funny ol' world this was turning out to be.

It wasn't long afterwards that Gwen decided to throw her bouquet. I decided to stand as far away as possible. There wasn't exactly much point in me catching it now, was there? Anyway, Ricki was the lucky girl who did get it, and she was ecstatic. It was hilarious. Good luck to her. Grayson looked quite amused too.

Before the bride and groom sped off to their hotel for the night (they were leaving for the States bright and early the next morning), I managed to have a quick word with them both. I told them to look after each other—and the little one in that belly of hers—and I explained what had happened with Grayson, and the fact that he was beginning to see me like a little sister anyway. They were pleased with the road I'd decided to take.

'You made a very grown-up decision there, girl, and it was the best one. You'll never get over Ryan with someone else in your way. Well, we have to go now. The car is waiting. Oh God, I love you, Summer, and I'm gonna miss you. We'll be back at the end of

September. You take care now,' Gwen said, getting a little teary. I hugged them both and let them say goodbye to the rest of their guests.

We all stood throwing more confetti and waved goodbye to the newlyweds as they drove off into the world of marriage. I cried again.

Grayson sneaked up behind me and told me I still had a big brother here in England.

I turned around and gave him a big hug, but told him to get back to the party. 'Go and enjoy yourself. A charming little woman is waiting for you inside there. Don't forget...she caught the bouquet, and you know what that means,' I laughed.

'Erm, that's a bit soon, don't you think?' he laughed. 'Aren't you coming back in?'

I shook my head. 'No, I'd rather head home.'

'Would you like me to drive you?'

'Don't be silly, you. Go on back to the party and enjoy yourself,' I said, and I gently pushed him in the direction of the reception.

He finally let me go, walking backwards with a grin before he turned and went back inside.

I managed to get a cab, and within an hour I was back home, enjoying a nice cup of tea, leafing through the photos of Portugal once again. Only this time, I was able to do it without feeling the slightest bit guilty.

CHAPTER 12

A few weeks had passed since Gwen's wedding, and I'd never felt so alone. Grayson had called numerous times to make sure I was okay, and I repeatedly told him I was fine. I lied. I wasn't fine at all.

I considered giving him a call, but I really didn't want to burden him with my problems. Besides, he and Ricki had been getting on like a house on fire, and I didn't want to cause any upset there.

Ricki had approached me at work and asked if I minded if she dated him. I'd laughed and said that we were very good friends but nothing else, and that I was really happy for them both. I wished them all the happiness in the world. Secretly, though, I wondered whether he'd told her about his mother.

Since I'd returned from Portugal, work had been peculiar. Mr Negativity had gradually turned into Mr Positivity: he appeared to be the happiest person in the office, which seemed to have a knock-on effect on everyone else there. Gavin had begun to dress better, and was starting to lose weight; I reckon he'd finally met a nice girl. I was pretty curious but didn't want to ask him, as I had no right interfering in his life like that.

Sadly, Jim's mother had been ill in hospital, so he'd taken some time off work to be with her. I got his contact details from Jack and sent flowers to his mum (even though I didn't know her) and a letter to Jim, hoping everything was going to be okay. He phoned me at the office to say thanks and to let me know his mum had been really impressed with the flowers, although lilies were perhaps a bit precipitant! I'd ordered them over the phone and, for some reason, the woman who took the order must have thought I was ordering for a funeral! Anyway, I apologised and explained I hadn't explicitly asked for lilies. But he and his mum had had a good laugh about it anyway, which had cheered her up. I laughed and suggested the three of us have dinner sometime when she was better.

Geoff Wankhorn was the only person in the office who hadn't really changed that much at all. He still managed to be a bit of a prick, but everybody else got on with their work and generally ignored him—which seemed to piss him off. Well, so it bloody should.

I was feeling so down that I actually decided to visit my mum, which I didn't do too often, for obvious reasons. When I arrived, though, she seemed genuinely thrilled to see me. Before going inside, I peered through the doorway to make sure no naked men were hiding under the coffee table or anything.

'Don't worry, sweetheart, there's no-one here but me. I've been meaning to give you a call, but I didn't think you'd really want to talk to me.'

'Why would you think that?'

She shrugged regretfully. 'Just the impression I get, that's all.'

Suddenly I felt awful. If she wanted me to feel guilty about being a cow sometimes, she'd certainly hit the nail on the head.

'Would you like a cup of tea and some cake? It's homemade.'

I stopped in my tracks. Mum never, ever, ever baked anything. 'Homemade? But you've never baked anything in your life. What's going on?'

'Well, I guess I'm finally settling down.' She shrugged again. 'Do you want some?'

'Of course. I'd love some. Wow. My mum bakes... I can't believe it!'

I sat in the lounge—desperately trying not to picture Jack on the coffee table—while she made the tea and brought it in with the most enormous, delicious-looking chocolate cake.

'Wow, Mum! This is amazing. This is what coming home to Mum should be like! Oh, sorry, I didn't mean it like that. You have your life. I have mine...like you've always said.'

'Summer, honey, don't be sorry. I know I've been a terrible mother, and you've been a not-so-great daughter, sometimes. That's life. But my life has changed a great deal over the past couple of months.'

'It has?' I asked with my mouth full of the best damn chocolate cake I'd ever tasted. She'd outdone herself, she really had.

'Yes, I've met someone really great. He's perfect for me, and I'm perfect for him. In fact, he wants us to move in together. That's why I was thinking of calling you. I guess I wanted to know what you thought.'

'You did?' I was gobsmacked. My mum never really wanted to know my opinion on anything, especially not concerning the decisions she was making in her life. 'Slow down, Mum. This is getting heavy.'

'No, darling. It's about time we sorted out our problems. Together. You are my daughter. I am your mother. I think it's about time we started to act like a family, for a change.'

I nodded. 'Okay. So who is this guy you're thinking of moving in with?'

'Jack Willoughby.'

'Bloody hell,' I coughed, spitting half a cup of tea and bits of cake all over the floor. 'Shit. Sorry.'

'Well I guess you don't approve then,' Mum said unhappily, as she went to get some kitchen roll to clear up the mess I'd made.

Wow. Shit. Bloody hell. So my mum was the reason Mr Negativity had changed his tune. I must admit I was quite impressed. And it must have been him that had made this profound change on her.

She came back into the room, looking sad.

'What's the matter, Mum?'

'I was hoping that you'd approve. But I guess that's asking too much.'

'But Mum, I do approve. I really do. I think it's great.'

I laughed as she looked up in shock. 'You do?'

'Sure. You wouldn't believe the effect you've had on Mr Negati —I mean... Jack. He used to be the world's most negative and miserable person. And in the space of a few months, he's actually become a complete pleasure to work with. And look at the effect he's had on you. He's turned you into a proper mum! I'm thrilled. Really I am. So when are you moving in together?'

My mum clapped her hands with joy and hugged me. 'Oh, thank you, darling. I don't think you realise how much your approval means to me. I can't wait to tell him.'

We smiled at each other and had some more cake.

'So you really made this yourself? I can't believe it.'

'Yes, I did, and I hadn't realised how much fun it could be. I've been going mad in the kitchen, making scones, biscuits, pies. You name it, I've probably made it. And...' she said, looking utterly impressed with herself, 'I'm actually quite good at it.'

I nodded and smiled, but my eyes must've given me away.

'Sweetheart, what's wrong? I mean, what's really wrong? I know I've never been one to give advice, but there's something really bothering you, isn't there? I'd really like to help...if you'll let me.'

I shook my head. I'd never even attempted to burden my mother with my troubles. Basically, she'd always been the last person I wanted to talk to, but it was different this time. She was different. 'Oh, Mum,' I whispered before unexpectedly bursting into tears.

She leaned forward and put her arms around me. For the first time, ever, I felt that I could tell her anything and everything. She didn't say a word; she just waited until I was ready to talk. All she did was hug me and stroke my hair. I felt so at ease. In fact, I felt like I'd finally come home.

And then I began to talk. I told her everything. Starting with meeting Grayson, to the trip to Portugal and Ryan, and my decision to end it there and then, and the Grayson thing again and Gwen's wedding. Everything. I didn't miss out a single thing. I cried in between and curled up on her sofa, my head leaning gently on her shoulder. She patiently listened without saying a word. And then, finally, when I finished talking, she just stroked my hair until I fell asleep.

A couple of hours later, I was awoken by the most delicious smell of something roasting in the oven. At first, I wondered where the hell I was and panicked, but when I heard Mum humming away in the kitchen, I dragged myself up and walked through.

'Oh, you're awake. I was just about to come and rouse you. Here,' she said, handing me a cup of tea.

'Thanks, Mum… I mean, really thanks…for listening.'

She smiled and patted my hand, 'That's what I'm here for, darling.'

I asked what she was cooking.

'A leg of lamb.'

Suddenly remembering Jack, I asked, 'I haven't ruined any plans you had with Jack today, have I?'

'He popped round when you were asleep. I told him you were here and he didn't want to intrude, so he left.'

I felt as if I'd ruined her day or something. 'I'm sorry. I can leave if you want him to come back.'

'Don't be silly. Besides, I told him we were doing a bit of 'mother and daughter bonding'—for the first time in our lives—and needed time to ourselves.' She smiled shyly.

I smiled too and asked if there was anything I could help her with. She handed me the peeler and some carrots while she cut up a cabbage and we talked about my work and Gwen's wedding.

But she soon put down the knife and said, 'Summer, I don't know if you really care about what I say, but I'm going to say it anyway.' She sat down at the kitchen table and asked me to sit, too. 'This boy, Ryan? Did you really love him?'

I wasn't entirely sure what to say. I mean, we'd only known each other two weeks, so how could it really have been love? It felt like love, but I wasn't sure, so that's what I told her.

She nodded. 'Do you feel the same now?'

'Yeah. I think I do.'

'But you've been trying to forget about him?'

changed a thing. The truth is, I made me the way I am by saying goodbye to Tristan. I should have told him I loved him.'

I stood up, walked round to the back of my mum's chair, and put my arms around her. 'You must have been through hell, and now I'm following in your footsteps,' I sighed.

'We are two very silly girls,' was all she said as she stood up and kissed my cheek. 'I'm sorry for not telling you sooner, perhaps it would have saved your relationship with Ryan.'

I shrugged my shoulders. 'Probably not. You weren't exactly in my good books. I probably wouldn't have listened. Or I would have done exactly the opposite of what you said. In the end, I chose to do what I did, and no-one would have made a difference.'

'Was this a gift from Tristan?' I asked, taking the brooch in my hand.

She nodded. 'I never wore it after he left.'

'Well I think you should wear it now, then,' I said, trying to pin it to her blouse, but she stopped me.

'No, it was a gift from your father, so you should have it. I want you to have it. Here, let me put it on you.'

I smiled and thanked her for such a meaningful gift. It was a simple round gold brooch with two diamonds in the middle. Mum sadly explained that when my dad had given it to her, he had said that the diamonds represented the two of them together, forever. It's something I would cherish. Always.

That evening, which had begun on such a lonely note, had become one of the most important days of my life. Not only had I been given my mum back, and my mum, her daughter, but I'd also learned the truth about my father. We had finally become a real family.

I realised my mum knew exactly what I was going through, and she said that she would always be there for me. No matter what. And that meant so much to me. I finally had someone who would help me get over the biggest mistake of my life.

CHAPTER 13

With a new lease of life and a spring in my step, I walked home that night feeling like a completely different woman. I'd left my flat alone and sorrowful, and I walked back in like someone new. I was finally prepared to really face the world. To begin again. To get on with it. To follow that yellow brick road. Okay, so maybe I was taking it a bit too far, but I felt good.

The first thing I did was take a couple of the photos of Ryan and me and put them in a frame and place them in the living room. I was ready to be asked about them. I was ready to talk about it. Yes!

Then I sat down and opened my mail, which had been mounting up the past couple of days. There was the usual crap: bills and statements, as well as a postcard from Gwen and Hugh. They were clearly having the time of their lives, and they'd sent the card from Las Vegas, where she'd lost a great deal of cash, but it hadn't mattered. It was fun, she wrote. They'd checked out the Grand Canyon. Awesome was her one word description of it. I looked forward to hearing all about it when they eventually got back.

Also in the post was a letter from my old school. Weird.

It turned out to be an invitation to a school reunion. My initial reaction was to dump it in the bin, but something stopped me, so I stood there staring at it for a while, thinking about it. Maybe it would be an excellent opportunity to help get my life back on track. I'd had a few school friends who I hadn't kept in touch with, so it would be fun to see what they were all doing with themselves. Unlike some of my friends, I hated social media—I never knew what to write, so I just didn't bother. Gwen was always trying to encourage me to get on Facebook and Twitter, but the idea made me cringe on the inside. I was way too boring for that stuff. I'm sure my old school pals were on there, but I'd managed until now without it, so why start?

Of course, if I did go to the reunion, I'd have to spend the next couple of weeks working out at the gym and going down to Alison's and Billy's to get myself sorted out. Maybe it would be good for me? So that was it. I decided to go for it. I would present a new me at that reunion. I grinned at myself in the mirror.

The date for the event was a Saturday in late September, and I would be there. I had two weeks to get ready. Gwen and Hugh were coming back the day after the reunion, so I'd have plenty of gossip to talk about. It was actually quite exciting.

oOo

THE FOLLOWING day was Monday morning, which, several months ago, I would have dreaded, but since Jack had turned over a new leaf, I actually looked forward to going to work.

The first thing I wanted to do was to have a private word with him, to congratulate him on his upcoming move to live with my mum. But when I got there, weirdly everyone in the office was smiling at me.

I hadn't got a clue what was going on, so I just went on, as usual, wishing them all a good morning.

Gavin, looking smart in jeans and a white shirt, came up to me and clapped me on the shoulder. 'Lucky cow,' he said with a huge grin. I frowned but smiled at the same time, marvelling that it was physically possible.

And then I was approached by Ricki, who squealed when she saw me. 'Oh, Summer, you must be so pleeaaased!'

I told her I hadn't got the foggiest idea what she was going on about and then, there on my desk, was an internal memo from the big boys upstairs:

Miss Summer Miller, please come and see me the minute you arrive.

William Shawshank

I gasped. What the hell was going on? Was I getting fired? But why would that make me a lucky cow, and why would I be so pleased? Something peculiar was going on, and clearly, nobody in the office was going to tell me what. I looked around to find Jack, but he was nowhere to be seen.

I nervously trundled up to the big man's office on the top floor; William Shawshank was the managing director of The News Corporation.

I approached his snotty-looking secretary, who looked at me over the top of her moon-shaped spectacles. 'May I be of any assistance?' she queried in a clearly put-on posh voice.

'Good morning. I'm Summer Miller. I received a memo from Mr Shawshank. He wants to see me,' I said, trying desperately hard not to appear in the least bit nervous. I failed miserably.

'Oh, yes, Miss Summer Miller. Just one moment please,' she said as she pressed the intercom to the big boss' office. 'Miss Summer Miller to see you, sir.'

I didn't hear what the response was, but she walked around her desk to a huge door to her left, knocked once and pushed it open.

'Mr. Shawshank will see you now, Miss Miller,' she said without even the briefest of smiles.

I politely thanked her and walked in.

'Miss Miller. Thank you for being so prompt.' As if I wouldn't be; I mean, this is the big boss man, for God's sake! 'You're probably wondering why you have been called up to see me?'

I gulped and nodded. 'Yes, sir. Mr Shawshank.' Your Highness?

'It has been brought to my attention that you have been doing a most excellent job down at the Gazette.'

It had? What on earth was going on?

'I realise this may sound a little odd, Miss Miller, but a position has arisen on our weekly England Probe magazine, and I would like you to consider yourself as a candidate for the job.'

I almost fainted. It was a bloody good job I was sitting down.

He smiled. A very kind smile. 'You're probably wondering why I am dealing with this matter and not the Personnel Department?'

Finally, I mustered up the courage to say something. 'Yes.' Well, it was the best I could do.

'I realise this is a bit of a shock. I assume you usually speak a little more?' he laughed.

He'd managed to break the ice.

'Yes, I'm sorry. It is a bit of a surprise. Something I certainly wasn't expecting. May I ask why I am being considered?'

'Of course. Over the past several months or so, I have been taking a great deal of notice of what has been going on downstairs,'—downstairs was an understatement, there were rather a lot of flights of them—'and I have been looking for the best page-maker, the one with the most flair. The most talented. Of course, I have spoken to the editors of each newspaper and magazine. You come highly recommended by your current editor, Jack Willough-by.' Surely he wasn't still desperate to get rid of me because of the coffee table thing? 'He tells me he thinks you're the best person for the job in the entire building.'

'May I ask when he told you this?'

'Let's see...' He buzzed his secretary. 'Miss McGurnstewart, please check my diary and find out when I had my last meeting with Jack Willoughby... Alright, thank you.' He looked back up at me. 'It was May 11th of this year.'

Well, now I was seriously gobsmacked. That was way before the coffee table/spanking incident. My God. I'd always assumed he hated me. Wow.

'Is there something wrong, Miss Miller?'

'No. Absolutely not, Mr Shawshank. I'm just thrilled. Totally thrilled.' I pulled myself together and tried to appear professional. 'I assume there are quite a few other candidates?'

'Actually no,' he grinned. 'In fact, I would like to offer you the position. Chief Pagemaker for the weekly England Probe. Naturally, the job entails a salary increase of...' He paused and looked briefly at some papers on his desk, appearing a trifle surprised at what he saw. 'Two-hundred per cent.'

This time I fell. I know I was sitting on the chair, but it made no difference. With a massive plod, my arse was on the floor. Shit. What a prat.

'Are you alright, Miss Miller?' he enquired as he peered over the desk.

I jumped up, attempting to be calm, my face crimson. 'Fine, fine. Fine, thank you.'

I planted my behind firmly on the chair again.

'Is that an acceptance, Miss Miller?'

I smiled, the grin reaching the far sides of my face. 'It is absolutely, completely and utterly an acceptance.'

'Excellent,' he said with his hand outstretched. I shook it firmly; I can't stand women with floppy handshakes. It's like meeting a wet fart. Not that I'd particularly like to meet a wet fart.

'It's wonderful to meet such a valued member of my staff, Miss Miller. And so nice that you can be yourself around me. So many of the people downstairs are tight-lipped—' And tight-arsed, in my opinion. But, of course, I didn't say that. '—and afraid to say what they mean. You, my dear, are a breath of fresh air. Welcome to the ladder of The News Corporation. Maybe, one day, you will be sitting in this chair, or possibly the floor beneath the chair.' He laughed heartily at his little joke.

I was told my new position would begin in a week. Excellent – that meant I had a great job title for my school reunion. There was only one thing missing from my life. Ryan. But there was nothing I could do about that. That was something I had to live without. Tough but true.

When I got back downstairs, I was greeted by applause from my colleagues. I smiled, laughed, curtseyed, saluted and...promptly fell down a flight of stairs.

Bloody hell! Everyone rushed over to see if I was okay; I was, and I wasn't. I was laughing at my so total humiliation in front of them all, but I was in pain. Serious pain. In fact, I thought I'd broken my leg.

'Summer, Summer. Are you alright?' it was Grayson.

I looked up from my rather unusual twisted position on the floor and tried to shake my head. I'd never broken anything before. It hurt. It really bloody hurt.

'I think we'd better get her to the hospital,' was all I heard before I went incredibly dizzy and blacked out.

CHAPTER 14

I woke up in a strange, overly-clean room, with bright white and snot-green walls. It was awful. I thought I was having a nightmare or something. The first thing I focused on looked like Jack. 'Jack? Is that you?'

'It's me, alright. How are you feeling?'

It suddenly occurred to me that I had excruciating pain in my ankle. 'Bloody hell. What on Earth happened?'

'Don't you remember?'

I shook my head.

'You fell down the stairs at the office. You broke your leg in three places,' he said, pointing to the enormous cast I was sporting on my left leg.

'Oh shit.'

Suddenly I remembered. I was trying to be cool about the promotion, waving, saluting, et cetera, and I fell. God, could I have been more embarrassing? I cringed.

'Apparently, you've become quite a star at the office. Congratulations on your promotion.'

'Thanks, Jack. I owe you. Mr Shawshank told me what you said. I'm really grateful,' I said with as much of a smile as I could muster under the circumstances.

'I told him you were the best because you are. I wasn't blowing sunshine up your arse for any other reason. You're the best person for the job, Summer.'

I smiled again. 'I also owe you congratulations'.

He looked at me quizzically.

'Mum told me.'

'How do you feel about that?'

'Honestly? I think it's fab. You make a great couple. You've both changed each other dramatically…for the better, too. I'm happy for you both.'

I could tell he really appreciated me telling him that.

'So what's going on here then? Aha, you've come to,' said a guy in a white smock-thing. Obviously the doctor. He approached me and pointed his little torch into my eyes.

'So how do you feel?'

'My leg is killing me, but apart from that—and the humiliation of falling down a flight of stairs in front of a crowd at the office—I don't feel too bad. I presume I can go home now?'

'Yes. There's no reason why you should stay here. Your leg is broken in three places, though, but they're pretty clean breaks, they should heal nicely. You blacked out from the initial pain then we had to knock you out to sort it out. It happens. It shouldn't happen again, though. Here's a prescription for some strong painkillers,' he said as he handed me the much-needed piece of paper.

'How long will I need the cast on for, Doctor?' I asked, hoping it wouldn't be long at all.

'Well, at least six weeks, possibly longer. You'll need crutches, which are here. But don't worry, you'll be fine. Take care. Good-bye,' and he waltzed out as quickly as he had waltzed in.

Six weeks. Shit. That meant I'd have to go the school reunion like this. Great.

'Darling! Darling! Are you alright? Oh dear. What on Earth happened?' Mum ran in and put her arms around me, and then she kissed Jack. They were so cute.

'I'm fine, Mum, honest. I just fell down some stairs, that's all.'

Jack nodded. 'I wasn't there at the time, but a couple of people in the office called me on my mobile to let me know she'd been brought here. I came straight here and then called you.'

I was surprised he'd dashed straight here. Actually, I was impressed; he was becoming a bit of a father figure, and when I told him with a grin, he blushed and squeezed my mum's hand.

She smiled and giggled. 'Sorry I couldn't get here any quicker. Work was hell today.'

Jack squeezed her hand.

'You didn't need to come, Mum. It's only a broken leg. But seeing as you're both here, are you guys gonna help me up and get me out of this horrible place, or what?'

oOo

THE NEXT DAY WAS A TUESDAY, and Jack had told me to take the day off work. He said I needed at least a day off to get over the shock. Of course, I took him up on that and stayed in bed until midday, when I was forced to get out of bed when there was a knock at the door.

'Hang on! I'll be right there. Sorry, I have a broken leg, and it takes a while to move,' I yelled as loud as possible.

After a few minutes of knocking everything over with the crutches, and hobbling along like an invalid (which I supposed I was), I managed to get to the door and open it.

'Miss…Summer Miller?' said a delivery boy as he checked his file.

'Uh-huh. That's me.'

'I have several deliveries for you.' He looked at my leg, smiled and said, 'I'll bring them inside, shall I?'

I nodded, wondering what on Earth it could be. I was too stupid to look at the van. If I'd noticed the flowers all over it, perhaps I'd have realised. Duh.

Anyway, in he came with rather a lot of bouquets. I signed for them, and he left.

Wow! There were loads.

I began to look at all the cards.

Have a nice trip? Sorry. Hope you're feeling better. Take care, Gavin. Oh, how sweet. My God.

Congratulations on the promotion. Sorry to hear about the fall, though. Get better soon. Call us. Jim and his mum. I laughed when I noticed the flowers were lilies.

Sweetheart. Call us if you need anything. We love you. Mum and Jack. They loved me; they were just too cute.

Dear Miss Miller. Terribly sorry to hear about your fall. I do hope it wasn't my fault for causing the excitement! Regards, William Shawshank. Wow, flowers from the Big Boss Man.

Look after that nice leg of yours! Get better soon. Call us. Luv Grayson and Ricki. So, they really were an 'us' then? Cool.

Naturally, there weren't any from Geoff Wankhorn. Not that I cared or anything.

CHAPTER 15

I decided to head to work the following day. There was little point staying home all day, doing nothing. Yeah, my leg still hurt like hell, but I had serious painkillers if I needed them. I could put myself to better use at the office. My only dilemma was how the hell was I going to get there? I supposed I could call a cab; I would soon be quite well off so it wasn't like I couldn't afford it or anything. But just as I was about to pick up the phone, it rang. It was Mum.

'Hi, sweetheart. You answered the phone quickly for someone who's on crutches, didn't you? How are you feeling, anyway?'

'Hi, Mum. Much better, thanks. I was just about to make a phone call to get a taxi to work.'

'What? You're going to work already?'

'Well there's not a lot of point hanging round here, is there? I know I can hardly walk, but there isn't really anything else wrong with me. I'm better off at the office.'

'Well, Jack has literally just left. I'll give him a quick buzz and see if he can pick you up. Don't call a taxi just yet. Wait five minutes or so, and I'll get him to ring you right back, okay?'

I nodded to myself and said, 'Okay. Oh, Mum…thanks for the flowers, it was lovely. Bye.'

I put the phone down and waited. It didn't take long for it to ring.

'Hi, Jack.'

'Good morning. I hope you're feeling better. Your mum says you want to go to work. Are you sure that's a good idea?'

I told him I was fine, really. So he said he'd be right round to pick me up. It was so great to finally have a kind of father figure in the family again. Again? What was I on about? There'd never been one. Okay, so it was great to have a father figure, full stop.

When we arrived at the office, everyone was surprised to see me back so soon. I thanked them for the lovely flowers, and they congratulated me properly on my promotion. All were eagerly wondering how the meeting upstairs went, so I said it was great although I fell off my chair once. They laughed, thinking I was joking, so I let it slide. After all, that was only my first fall that day; the second fall broke my bloody leg. I guess I looked like a complete idiot. A major prat. That was just me.

I also called Jim to thank him for the lilies; what a lovely thought and what beautiful funeral flowers. I'd laughed and told him, fortunately, it wasn't that bad a fall. Just a broken leg—albeit in three places. He explained his mother was quickly recovering and would be out of hospital soon. He was pleased to hear from me, and we said again that we'd have to have dinner when she was on the up. I told him I looked forward to it, said goodbye and put the phone down. He was a sweetie.

That day went by quickly, with everybody fussing over me and bringing me tea and coffee all day long. Grayson and Ricki even brought me lunch from McDonald's, which was very sweet. He'd remembered what I'd eaten a few months ago. Chicken nuggets and a strawberry milkshake—my favourite—which I consumed in less than five minutes. Yummy.

Jack dropped me off home, making sure I was alright and not leaving until I was safely inside the flat. 'Are you sure you're okay? Your mum…and me, of course, worry about you, y' know?'

'Jack. Honestly, I'm fine, and I'll be fine. It's only a broken leg. Now, shoo, go on. Mum's probably waiting for you. In fact, isn't today the official day?'

Jack nodded and said she was packing, literally as we spoke.

She was starting the move in with him that very day. I told him to beat it, so he said goodbye and left.

I was all on my lonesome once again, so I made a nice cup of tea and hobbled into the living room, where I had a quick look at the photos of Ryan and me before I sat down and switched on the TV. I must have dropped off because I suddenly woke up with something wet on my lap. Shit. It was my tea. Luckily it was stone cold, but I'd managed to pour half a cup down my skirt and on the sofa. It was a good job my leg was in an elevated position; otherwise, it would have dribbled into the cast. That would have been lovely.

I got up as quickly as I could and tried to remove my skirt. It was amazing how difficult it was to get on with ordinary life with a great big white hunk of cement-like stuff stuck to your leg. My balance had gone entirely to shit.

After a ten-minute struggle, I finally managed to get it off. I was just heading to the kitchen to get a cloth to wipe the sofa when the phone rang.

Grayson sounded cheerful. 'Hello! How is it going? Are you alright?'

'Well, It's tougher than I thought it would be, but I'm managing okay. So, what's up?'

'Does there have to be anything wrong for me to call a good friend?'

'Sorry. I guess not.'

'Are you alone?' he asked.

I nodded to myself again and sighed. 'Yeah'.

'Well from that sound, I guess you'd like some company. How about I come round with pizza or something?'

I smiled. 'That would be fab'.

Half an hour later, he was knocking at the door with a bottle of wine and a pizza.

'Pizza Delivery!' he yelled as I hobbled to unlock the door.

'Hello you,' I said as he kissed me on the cheek.

'So how come you're not with Ricki tonight?'

'She's having a talk with her parents,' he replied with a semi-serious look on his face.

'God. That sounds ominous. What's that all about?' I knew Ricki still lived at home with her mum and dad, so it could have meant anything.

We sat down on the couch as he opened the wine and poured two glasses. I probably shouldn't have been drinking with the painkillers...but what the hell.

'Well she's telling them that she's moving out,' he stopped and smiled, 'and...is moving in with me.'

Wow. That didn't take them long, did it? I hoped they weren't rushing in too fast. I kind of felt responsible, because it was me who'd pushed them together in the first place.

'There's no need to worry, Summer. We've really hit it off, thanks to you. She even knows about my mum. In fact, I introduced them the other day.'

'Wow. It didn't take you long, did it? How did that little meeting go?' I asked, stuffing a slice of pepperoni pizza into my mouth, mozzarella slowly dribbling down my chin.

'Actually, it went well. Mum was thrilled to finally meet a friend of mine. I told her we were thinking of moving in together, and she totally understood. She even said she'd remove all her girlie things from my place just so Ricki didn't feel uncomfortable with it,' he laughed. 'Ricki likes her. She accepts what she does for a living... She doesn't really like it, but she accepts it.'

I nodded, understanding exactly what she meant.

He stood up and wandered around the room, 'So, I guess this is...Ryan, isn't it?'

'Yup.' I wasn't sure how he'd react at seeing the photos, so I just waited quietly.

'He's a good looking guy.' He smiled at me. A smile with genuine concern behind it, 'You really miss him, don't you?'

I looked away from him. I still cried every now and again, whenever the subject came up.

'Summer. You know you can talk to me. We've already been through all this. Remember? Sis?'

I smiled again, remembering our words at Gwen's wedding. I'd been so worried about hurting him, but his feelings had already changed towards me. We'd become more like brother and sister than boyfriend and girlfriend. I knew that I could talk to him and that he was there for me, but…about Ryan?

'You don't have to talk about it if you don't want to. I can see how much it hurts. It's written all over your face. In fact, if I look close enough, there's a sign on your forehead…' he said, squinting and scrutinising my face. 'And it says, "I am afraid to talk about Ryan because I still love him. A lot. A real lot".'

I laughed and pushed him away. 'Okay, okay. You're right. I miss him like crazy, and I guess I'm madly in love with him, but slowly, very slowly, I think I'm getting over him.'

He shook his head. 'I don't think so, but if that's what you want to keep telling yourself, then so be it.'

I didn't want to talk about it anymore, so I reverted the subject back to him and Ricki, which suited Grayson just fine. He thought the world of her and loved to talk about her. At that moment, she was obviously his favourite subject.

He left a few hours later and headed home while I struggled to have a bath. Eventually, I managed quite successfully, actually. In other words, my cast remained dry while my bathroom floor resembled a swimming pool. I couldn't be bothered to try and dry it off, so I just left it. I was sure it'd be dry by the morning.

Just before I climbed into bed, the phone rang. An odd time to be ringing, but I stumbled over to it and picked it up. There was an echo on the line. 'Summer—Summer, it's Gwen—it's Gwen. How are you doin'—How are you doin'?'

I was thrilled to hear from her, although it was a bit on the strange side why she was calling me all the way from America when she was literally coming home that weekend.

'Gwen! It's great to hear from you. I'm sorry, but there's an echo on the line, and I can't hear you very well,' I yelled down the line as if I was shouting to her across the ocean.

'Well I can hear you perfectly—well I can hear you perfectly. Listen—listen. What have you been up to—What have you been up to?'

What a weird phone call. Surely she could ask me all this on Sunday?

I told her everything that had been going on anyway. Maybe

she really missed me and needed to talk to make sure I was doing okay, so I explained that I was going to the school reunion on Saturday afternoon, so I was alright, I had something to plan for.

'Are you sure you're okay? You still sound unhappy. Do you still miss Ryan?'

I told her of course, and she said, 'Okay, never mind then, honey. Everything is going to be okay. Bye then.'

Everything was going to be okay, was it? Well, if she said so. Maybe she was drunk. No, not with the pregnancy. I shrugged, put the phone down, and wondered what time it was in America.

Then, yawning, I climbed into bed and fell into a lovely deep sleep. Not without thinking of Ryan first, though. I wondered what he was doing. I tried hard not to wonder whether he had found someone new, but I couldn't help it. Secretly, I hoped he hadn't, even though I was always going on about how he deserved someone better than me.

Ryan… Ryan… Ryan. The love of my life. My final thoughts before sleep.

CHAPTER 16

There were a few days left until the school reunion, although on occasion I had considered not bothering with it. I figured I'd look a bit of a prat, hobbling in with my leg in such a state, but after giving it some serious thought, I came to the conclusion that it wasn't such a bad idea after all. Especially considering I could boast about me being the new chief page-maker for the England Probe magazine. It was quite a popular mag, after all.

But I couldn't boast about having some gorgeous hunk of a boyfriend, husband, fiancé, or whatever. Perhaps I should have hired someone for the day. One of those really sexy smooth gigolo types. Tongues would certainly wag. Mine included. Actually, I tell a lie. I would be miserable with any bloke, with one exception, of course—but that goes without saying.

I had planned on spending a great deal of time before the reunion being pampered and attempting to beautify myself. Unfortunately, I hadn't really had the chance, what with the fall and the broken leg and all.

With just a couple of days left, I decided to get as much pampering done as humanly possible. So I called on the services of my good friends Grayson and Ricki, who drove me downtown to see first George, and then Alison and Billy.

As I went in to see George, I told them I wouldn't be long, so they waited for me in the car.

George was pleased to see me.

'Summer Miller, how wonderful to see you! How are you? And how is the lovely Gwen? Have you been back to the club since, for some good stripping fun? What on Earth are you doing here? What in heavens happened to your poor leg?' he giggled as he air kissed my cheeks.

I laughed. 'It's good to see you too, George.' He helped me sit down, and I continued, 'Gwen and Hugh are fine. They're still on honeymoon at the moment, but they're coming back this weekend. How are you?'

'I'm great. Absolutely great…but go on, tell me all the gossip,' he said as he clapped his hands in excitement.

'Well, there's not much to tell, really. Apart from the fact that I broke my leg falling down the stairs at the office. It was mortifying…and no, I haven't been back to the club.' I smirked. 'But I am going to a school reunion on Saturday, and I could really use your advice…seeing as you're the expert.'

This comment brought a smile to his face and caused his cheeks to turn a dark crimson colour. 'Of course, I would love to help you, but how can I?'

I explained that I wanted to look as great as physically possible on Saturday and I didn't know what to wear. 'Any ideas?'

Clapping his hands with excitement once again, he exclaimed, 'Oh! I see! Well, let me look at you… hhmmm… yes, I see, yes, beautiful… possible… maybe…'

'I'm sorry, George, but I really can't stay too long, friends are waiting for me in the car,' I apologised.

'Oh, that's okay,' he replied, looking slightly disappointed. Maybe I shouldn't have bothered. I mean, I was 24, for God's sake, surely I should know what suited me by now. But what the heck, I wanted a professional opinion, and George was that professional. Not only did he make clothes, but he also designed them to suit you, and he was an expert on colour.

'Okay. If I were you, I'd wear white. You still have a nice tan, and white would show that off to its limit. I would have said a white trouser suit, but that's possibly a little difficult now,' he said, pointing to my leg.

I nodded.

'So, a white dress? A white skirt suit? Something that skims the body as opposed to clings? Anything like that, really—it will make you beautiful. I guarantee it.'

I smiled happily. I did have a couple of white things I could wear.

I kissed George on both cheeks and thanked him for his help. I offered to pay for his advice, but he wouldn't let me.

'No, don't be silly! Instead, you can take me to that club again,' he said with an excited wink.

I laughed and nodded in agreement, and then hobbled out onto the street back to the car. Grayson and Ricki both hopped out the second they saw me (as if I was utterly incapable of looking after myself) and helped me in.

We drove round to Alison's salon, and I told them I'd get a cab home later. They were a bit worried, but I basically told them they had no choice.

They eventually gave in, and I thanked them profusely for chauffeuring me before waving from the pavement.

'Oh. My. God. What on Earth happened to you?'

'Well, that's a bit of an embarrassing story...'

'All the more reason to hear it, then,' interrupted Alison, ever the typical hairstylist who just loves a bit of gossip.

So I told her and Billie all about my morning several few days ago. It didn't take long for them to be practically rolling around on the floor at my expense. The other clients in the salon had found it rather amusing too. Okay, I admit, I did exaggerate it to my bene-fit, but I loved to get people laughing, and it was usually due to an injury I had sustained or an embarrassing situation I had got myself into—which tended to happen slightly more often than not.

Clearly impressed by the tale, and finally a bit calmer after their little outbursts of hysterics, they began to take a look at me to see what could be done. I had already explained on the phone that I wanted to look like a new woman for this reunion. Quite how they were going to create this super-babe, I had no idea. After all, my hair was already pretty short, so I couldn't exactly go for a brand new cut or anything like that.

'How about colouring your hair?' mumbled Alison as she looked at me in the mirror, walking from one side to the other to check out my profile.

'Hmmm. We could go really wacky and go bright red,' she scratched her head like Laurel—or was it Hardy? Either way, it was way before my time.

'Ah. I've got it…extensions. We could give you majorly long hair. It'd look great. What d'ya think?'

'Well, I don't really know, Ali. It's a bit drastic, isn't it? And apart from that, it's bloody expensive, isn't it? And doesn't it take absolutely ages and ages? Time is one thing I haven't exactly got. I mean, I have to work tomorrow, and the reunion is the day after,' I moaned.

'Nah. It's not that expensive.' Then she whispered so that her other clients wouldn't hear, 'I'll give you a good price, don't you worry about that.' She winked at me and continued, 'I'm quite happy to work late tonight. Oh, shit, I can't tonight. Steve's expecting me back early. But I can tomorrow. I'll come round to your place if you want, that way you haven't got to worry about getting a lift in with that leg of yours. What do you reckon?'

I liked the idea of her coming to me for a change, but about the extensions, I really wasn't so sure. It'd been years since I had long hair. 'It won't look like horse hair or something, will it?'

Shaking her head, she told me not to be so stupid. 'I promise you, it will look totally natural. Promise. Honest. Cross my heart.'

'Why are you so keen to do it, anyway?'

'Because,' interrupted Billy, 'she's never done it before. She's been waiting for a guinea pig.'

'Et voilá! One guinea pig, coming right up,' laughed Ali nervously as she looked right at me.

I really wasn't sure, but I've always been game for a laugh, so why the hell not? Ali beamed in delight, her eyes wide like mine had been when I'd gyrated with Scott the male stripper. Bloody hell, I'd remembered his name. Shit. I didn't want to remember his name. I didn't want to remember anyone's name. Okay, maybe one incy, wincy, tiny, little exception.

'So you're going to be messing with my hair tomorrow evening, so what about right now? I don't want to have been driven all the way down here for nothing. How about a facial, Billy? Or do you want to come round tomorrow night too? We could get some food and drink in... Not too much drink, though... especially not you, Ali, I don't want to end up looking like a bloody scarecrow or something,' I laughed nervously.

They agreed it was a great idea, so we arranged for them to come round to my flat at six the following night. I offered to get the food and stuff, but they wouldn't have it.

'No, we'll get some on the way over. Besides, how exactly would you have gone out to get it? You'd have walked a couple of miles on your crutches, would you? We'll bring it.'

They were so right, of course. I kept forgetting about my leg, although how I was managing to do that, I've no idea. How does one forget about a cumbersome heavy cast, which prevents one from carrying out one's everyday life? This one doesn't have the foggiest idea.

I hung around the salon for half an hour, until the cab I'd called arrived, and then sped off in the direction of my place. The rest of the evening was spent flicking through magazines looking at people's hair. I wondered how I was going to look after this so-called miraculous transformation. I wished I was as confident as Ali and Billy.

I didn't really have the slightest idea how it was going to look. Would it be long and curly, like Cher's in Mermaids—gosh, that must have been one old magazine. I rather liked that hairdo though, although it probably wasn't quite me. So, to find out, I found a small photo of me and cut out my face, placing it on top of Cher's. Er, no, definitely not.

I continued flicking through magazines and putting my photo on others.

How about Scary Spice? Ha Ha! Having a laugh.

Jennifer Lopez? Not quite. I guess I was destined to be blonde. Brown did not suit me at all.

Ah, Nicole Kidman in Moulin Rouge. Now that looked rather nice. In fact, it was me. Without a doubt. Perfect. I would show the picture to Ali and see what she had to say about it.

Knowing my luck, she was probably thinking more on the lines of Slash from Guns' n'Roses. At least it'd cover my face. I'd need to buy some smokes for that look though.

God, I was becoming increasingly sad. 'Gwen, come back... pleeease. Save me from this insanity that is boredom and loneliness,' I murmured into the empty flat, flipping the magazine shut.

oOo

THE FOLLOWING day was my last day at the Gazette, and even Geoff was acting relatively pleasant towards me. Maybe he wanted my old job? I hadn't even considered what would happen in that respect. It hadn't even crossed my mind who would be doing what I'd been doing for the past year or so. Not that it was a position better than anyone else's in that area. It wasn't. It was a step up from running errands and making tea and coffee, though. Maybe Ricki would get it. I decided to ask Jack about that. I'd put in a good word if she wanted me to.

Apparently, they were all sad to see me go but wished me the best of luck upstairs.

'Don't forget us minor souls down here, now that you're rubbing shoulders with the Big Boss Man,' said Gavin. 'Come down and say hi, every now and again. We... We'll ...miss you.'

Aw, that was so sweet. I was surprised they'd all liked me so much. Probably because I gave them such great entertainment, what with me crashing cars and falling downstairs all the time. Okay, maybe not all the time, but often enough.

'Thanks, Gavin. But I'm only upstairs, exactly where you'll be soon, I'm sure. Take care of yourself. Bye, everyone. Take care. It's been great working with you all,' I yelled as I tried hard to climb up the stairs, using the bannister one side and a crutch on the other.

The crutch I wasn't using was swinging about hitting everybody as I hobbled.

'Oops, sorry. Mind the... crutch... sorry. Ouch. Er, careful. Hopalong Summer coming through... lookout.'

I turned to say one final farewell, 'Goodbye, salut, arrivederci, ciao, sayonara!' I laughed, but not a single person was looking at me.

There I was. A total prat again. But they weren't watching, so I guess I was the only one thinking I was a prat for a change.

Grayson had very kindly taken me home, wishing me a great weekend as I hobbled (I was doing an awful lot of hobbling lately) into the flat. I returned the wish with a wave and a cheeky smile. He was taking Ricki away for a 'dirty weekend' apparently, but she didn't know it was going to be a mucky one. He'd told me in utmost secrecy. I'd had great difficulty not mentioning it to her, though. I was such a terrible gossip but was pretty proud of myself that I'd managed to keep schtum.

Ali and Billy arrived dead on six, with takeaway fish'n'chips from the local chippie. It smelled divine. After eating, we got down to business. Ali thought my picture of my face with Nicole Kidman's hair was highly amusing.

'I want to look like this,' I'd said, proudly pointing to it. 'Make me a glamour puss, like that.'

She sniggered, which I chose to ignore. I wanted to be beautiful. So I left them to pamper away as I drifted into the wonderful world of my imagination. Of course, it hadn't been that imaginative lately, all I'd been thinking about was Ryan this, Ryan that, and Ryan here and Ryan there. I completely relaxed, thinking about that wonderful massage he'd given me when I'd hurt my back, only to be plucked out of the memory when Ali literally started 'plucking'. Or should I say yanking? 'Bloody hell! You could have warned me!'

'Er, actually, sweetheart, I did—a couple of times. You seemed to be in a world of your own. I thought you were sleeping with your eyes open. These are serious eyebrows, girl. When on Earth did you last do them?'

'Er, probably quite a few months ago.'

'It shows. You look like Madonna in Who's That Girl.'

'Madonna looked fantastic in that film.'

'Yeah, but not her eyebrows. Rather on the bushy side.'

'Maybe that was cool back then. It was quite a long time ago. In fact, that was the mid-eighties, wasn't it?'

They both nodded.

'If you really wanted to insult me, you could have said my eyebrows looked like that girl's from Baywatch.'

'Baywatch?'

'Yeah, you know... Baywatch... babes and dudes on the beach saving people from drowning and stuff?'

'Summer, if I didn't know you, I'd say you were forty, not twenty-four!' chuckled Billy.

'You mean Pamela Anderson?' asked Ali curiously.

'You mean you know the show too?' Billy asked, curiously.

'It's not that old,' Ali smiled.

'No, silly, not Pamela. The other blonde bombshell... er, shit, what was her name? Oh, you must know. She was in that film with Steven Seagal, too. Y'know, the one on the navy ship where she jumps out of the cake, showing off her big boobs... enormous boobs, more like.'

'Steven Seagal? Who's that?'

'Oh Billy, you haven't lived if you haven't seen any Steven Seagal movies,' I laughed.

'Yeah, I remember that film Summer. Erica something or other, wasn't it? And her boobs weren't enormous. Yours are just small, that's all,' quipped Ali.

'Thanks so much for reminding me,' I mumbled. 'Am I beautiful yet?'

Both of them shook their heads a bit too vigorously for my liking, but I'd given them the job, and I was enjoying the pampering.

I didn't even ask how the hair was going to be; I didn't dare. If it were really awful, I'd simply ask her to chop it all off again. An expensive haircut, I know. But I wasn't going to this thing the next day looking like the abominable snowman.

'Erica Eleniak! That's it. That's the Baywatch babe's name,' shouted Ali half an hour later. We'd all gone back into our own little worlds again, so Billy and I half jumped out of our skins.

'Ali, you scared the living daylights out of us. This waxing takes a lot of care and attention. I wouldn't want to mess it up for Summer. She'd probably never speak to me again.'

I whispered, 'Too right,' and winced when Billy ripped off the wax from my lower leg. God, I hated having my legs done. It was such a shitty thing to do, but it was more convenient than shaving, and even though it hurt like hell, I'd begun to get used to the pain. I remembered the first time I'd ever used anything like that. It had been one of those machines that pulled the hair out. On the box, it had said 'painless hair removal'. Figuring it sounded pretty good, I gave it a go. Jesus Christ. Pain. Absolute pain. Complete and utterly unbelievable, awful pain. The second time I tried it, I'd drunk a couple of tumblers of brandy first, and a friend had even given me a cigarette. It hadn't really hurt at all. In fact, it had been quite a pleasant experience. Later I found out, it hadn't been a cigarette at all… it had been a spliff. I'd been furious. Mind you, at least it had stopped the pain.

Since then, I'd had my legs waxed by a professional, and the agony had been reduced significantly. Billy was an expert at that sort of thing, and the important thing was to trust the person carrying out the feat. And a feat it certainly was. And at least this time there was only one leg exposed to be waxed.

After my leg and armpits were done, my facial completed, spots squeezed, hands manicured and feet pedicured, I was slowly feeling beautified, like a new woman. My head, though, seemed to be feeling heavier and heavier.

'This so-called hair is bloody heavy isn't it?'

'Don't be silly. It's coz you're not used to it. Plus, the fact that I've been pulling your hair this way and that for several hours doesn't help.'

'How does it look?'

I watched Billy look at Ali, and they quickly looked away from each other. Kind of like they were suppressing the urge to laugh. Oh, God. I hoped not.

'Weeellll???'

'Great. Just great,' quipped Ali.

I didn't say a word. I just let her get on with it.

Finally, a few hours later, after watching TV while Ali continued working on my hair, she'd finished.

'Okay, Summer. I'm done.'

I was excited but nervous at the same time. Actually, I was scared shitless. I was petrified I was going to look like one of those really weird surfer-types with long hair that looks like it's never actually been washed.

Slowly I stood up, with their much-needed help. To the best of my ability, I limped towards the mirror, which loomed ominously above the fireplace. This is it, I thought. The moment I'd been waiting for.

I closed my eyes as I approached and then stopped. My heart thudded heavily in my chest. This was it. Do or die. I opened one eye, but couldn't see without the other one, so I opened that one too. I gasped.

The girls fell about laughing.

'Hee hee! We fooled you! We fooled you! You fell for it! You thought we were sniggering and smirking at it all night when really… When really it looks gorgeous. You look like a princess or something,' they laughed.

Wow. I was amazed at the transformation. I looked like someone else. It just didn't look like me at all. Summer Miller. That wasn't Summer Miller looking back at me. Who was it? Cor, if I was a bloke! Even I was impressed.

'Jeeze, Ali. Wow. Well here's your guinea pig,' I shrieked, attempting to jump up and down with excitement, but ended up half in a pile on the floor.

'Ooh, that must have hurt,' said Billy as she rushed to help me back onto the chair.

But I was fine. I was always falling. Although, my inner thighs felt a bit over-stretched; I'd had to do a kind of splits because of the cast. God, I badly needed my yoga class. But I guess that would be a tad tricky with this cumbersome thing to contend with.

'I'd like to take some photos to show prospective clients. Would you mind?' asked Ali.

'Of course not, but I'd rather not tonight. It's really late, and I've got bags the size of dustbin lids under my eyes. How about this weekend? Is that okay?'

She smiled and nodded happily as I pulled myself up from the chair to get another look at this beauty in the mirror.

I had long blonde hair down my back. It appeared to have a great deal of oomph and bounce, and it softened my face so much that I could easily pass for someone else... Scarlet Johannsen for instance? Amber Heard? Okay, so I was having a bout of wishful thinking. But I did look good... Well, I did providing I didn't look too closely at the mirror, and I didn't yaaaaaaaaaawwwwwnnnnn.

The girls were so impressed by the evening's work that they left with huge smiles on their faces and suggested I paid them the next time I was in town. Did that mean they didn't want to bring me back to reality with too much of a thud? I hoped not, for my piggy bank's sake.

I had a quick bath—if you could call it quick, considering not only did I now have to deal with a cement leg but I also had to prevent getting my long locks wet, too. I pretty much managed but was absolutely and totally exhausted by the time I'd finished.

My bed was heaven-sent that night. I snuggled up warm and cosy, and then remembered I needed to put on my alarm clock. I didn't want to wake up really late. The cab was booked for midday.

So I snuggled up once again and slowly began to drop off to sleep. Not without thinking my usual wonderful night-time thoughts first though, of course. Ryan and Summer here. Ryan and Summer there. Ryan and Summer everywhere. Mmmmmm. Night night, Ryan...darling.

CHAPTER 17

Saturday finally arrived, and I climbed out of bed, feeling absolutely fantastic. I really felt like a new woman.

I went into the bathroom and stood looking in the mirror. My hair looked amazing. I looked great; a bit too great for someone who had a broken leg, a broken heart, and who'd just got up. Oh well. I didn't think anything of it, except it was just a tad strange. Usually, I fell out of bed feeling like shit and looking like shit. Why today was so different God only knew. Why, God? No answer. Never mind.

Anyway, I ran a bath and went back into my bedroom and put on my satin ivory robe—what on Earth was I doing and why did I feel sooo goooood? I put on some music while I glided around the flat on a high. I took out a flute glass and poured myself some champagne and orange juice. An odd thing to do on a Saturday morning, but I did it nonetheless. It tasted divine.

I hummed along to Barbra Streisand's Woman In Love (how peculiar—I seemed to know the words, even though I'd never really listened to it before) as I flicked through a Country Homes magazine (I didn't recall buying that. Usually I stuck to Cosmo).

I heard the postman pop some post through the letterbox, so I glided through to the front door to see if there was anything interesting. Just a postcard from Gwen and Hugh in Australia...

Australia? I thought they'd gone to America? I shrugged and continued to see what else there was. Another postcard, this time from Bradley Cooper. I smiled. How sweet of him to think of me. And a love letter from Ryan Gosling, pledging his undying love and attention to me, always. Oh, how lovely.

I headed back into the kitchen and poured myself another Bucks Fizz and then walked out on to the balcony to see what the weather was doing. It was blissfully hot, and the sky was bluer than blue. Excellent. A perfect day for a reunion.

Suddenly I heard the letterbox go again. I curiously wandered back inside to see what it was all about.

There was a single red rose lying on the floor by the door.

I smiled, picked it up and smelled it. Mmm. Beautiful. It didn't even occur to me to see how it had got there. That kind of thing happened all the time. Possibly one of my many admirers. As I turned, I heard the letterbox flip once again. This time there was an envelope on the floor. Opening it, it read:

Darling, I Miss You.

I giggled. Sweet. How sweet. Again I didn't open the door.

Another envelope appeared.

Darling, I Love You.

And another one.

Darling, Will You Be My Wife?

Finally, I slowly opened the door. The slight breeze opened my robe, revealing my sexiest underwear and slim toned body to the man at the door. My long hair blew in the wind.

Ryan.

'Darling, Ryan. How I missed you so,' I whispered as the love of my life took me in his arms and kissed me hard on the lips.

'Summer, dearest. You look positively stunning. A true English rose. Will you marry me?'

'Oh yes, oh, yeeees. Of course I'll marry you,' I said as we turned to go back into the flat. I noticed my bath was overflowing, and the water was running down the stairs and leaking from the ceiling. But it didn't matter. Ryan was here. Ryan was with me. Ryan was mine, all mine.

Rudely interrupting us, the phone began to ring.

Ryan looked at me.

'No darling, just ignore it. Whoever it is, they don't matter. It's just you and me now,' I said with a smile.

But he shook his head at me, even as he faded away.

'Noooooooooooooooo!' I wailed as I woke up with a start, the alarm buzzing and buzzing, and buzzing some more.

Fuck, fuck, fuck! I'd been dreaming. It was all one big dream. One big, wonderful, amazing dream. Ryan had come back for me. I sobbed and sobbed as I threw the alarm clock to the floor on the other side of the room.

Forgetting about my leg, I attempted to climb out of bed. When I realised, it was too late. There was a huge thud, and I was in a heap on the carpet. Again. Thank God I had a rug. That would have been extremely painful on tiles. Still, it hurt enough, and it took me ages to try and get back up again. Finally, I sat on the bed for a minute or two before trying to stand up again. I grabbed my crutches and hobbled into the bathroom.

Standing in front of the mirror, I noticed I had big black bags under my eyes, my lips seemed to be twice their usual size (that happened to me in the mornings sometimes), and I had a nice big spot on the end of my nose. To top it all off, my long locks didn't look half as good as they had the night before. In fact, they looked a mess. Great. I was going to look like one of Cinderella's ugly stepsisters when I had planned to look like Cinderella herself. The belle of the ball. Huh! What a joke. I was depressed. I looked like shit, and I felt like shit. What a horrible start to the day.

As I perched on the edge of the bath and turned on the tap, I remembered some of the details of my dream and laughed to myself. Yeah right. If only.

Prancing around in some silk negligee drinking champagne first thing in the morning and getting post and love letters from Bradley Cooper and Ryan Gosling. It had been a fantastic dream, though. I couldn't complain about that. I wondered if there was some kind of drug I could take that would leave me in a permanent dream state? Like something out of The Matrix? Perhaps I was dreaming now, and in real life, I was beautiful and had dates with the stars. Dream on, Summer.

I waited for the bath to run—there was no point leaving the bathroom because it took so long to move with the cast on my leg. I took off my seriously old dull brown pyjamas and knickers. No, my knickers were not brown. But that's when I noticed... my period had arrived. Oh, for God's sake. Of all days, it had to come on the one day that I'd been looking forward to for some time. It did explain the zit, though. The one day I was supposed to look and feel beautiful. The one day I was supposed to show up all my old school mates. Now I couldn't wear white. Well, I could, but... what if something happened? What if I leaked or something? And worse still, what if I leaked and I didn't know? Jesus. I'd be walking around with a great big red stain on my behind. Actually, worst case scenario, what if...the blood went a bit brown (like it often does) and I leaked? Everyone would think I'd pooed myself!! Oh God. Definitely not wearing white.

So what the hell was I going to wear? Shit, I hadn't even thought about my period arriving. If I had, I would have asked George if he'd any other alternatives for me.

I pushed my PJs and underwear to one side and climbed into the bath like some sort of lumbering oaf. Of course, I managed to get water all over the bathroom floor again. I wondered if I was going to do that every single bath time until the cast came off.

The hot water instantly had an effect on me, though. It felt good. Almost as good as a full body massage. Okay, maybe not. But it was good. I sank down, carefully keeping my leg hoisted up out of the water, and suddenly remembered my hair. Shit. I jumped and grabbed it, holding it on top of my head while I looked around to see if there was anything I could tie it up with. Something I hadn't thought of when Ali had been doing it. Well, why would I? I'd had short hair for years. My eyes settled on a sock on the floor, which I could just about reach with the loofah. It was dirty but not that dirty, so I ingeniously used it as a scrunchie, tying it together and then winding my hair round and round in a kind of knot and securing it with the sock. Cool. I felt like MacGyver.

A couple of hours later I was ready, although I didn't feel like the beauty I'd hoped I would.

Because I could no longer wear white, I settled for a long

maroon dress I'd forgotten existed. Not exactly ultra-fashionable, but it fitted nicely, so it just had to do. I would have worn trousers but under the circumstances, well... that just wasn't possible. I would have had to cut up one leg to fit my cast into it, and I wasn't that desperate. I would have also liked to wear my favourite black strappy sandals, but they were a bit high, and I'd probably fall over, considering I could only wear one, so I put on my black flats instead. I wore my new hair down... I didn't have much choice, really. Unless I wanted to wear a dirty sock in it. Er, no.

I used my favourite make-up to accentuate my best features. Okay, so I didn't have any best features, so I settled on what I always wore, brown eye-shadow, black mascara, a touch of brown eyeliner, a little pinky-brown blusher and pale pink lipstick. It did the job, anyway.

The cab arrived ten minutes late, just as I was beginning to panic. I certainly didn't want to be the last person to arrive. People would stare at me anyway, let alone the last lonely single person falling in with one dodgy leg. At least if I was there a bit earlier, I could find a good spot to try and blend in...if that was at all physically possible. Worth a try in my book, though.

The cabbie nattered away, and I just smiled and nodded; I wasn't particularly in the mood to make meaningless conversation with a little fat Londoner with no teeth, who I hoped I'd never come across again.

The reunion was taking place at a local hotel, in the gardens of Hotel Bushenkel, as it stated in the invitation. It was lucky it wasn't raining, although peering out of the window the weather did appear a tad on the dreary side. Well, that was nothing new really, was it? I sat back and thought of the glorious weather back in Portugal and then remembered the previous night's dream. The weather had been gorgeous there too.

We pulled up outside the hotel, so I paid fatso and clambered out without the slightest bit of elegance. In fact, I even flashed my knickers; how, I've no idea. I was wearing a long dress. I entered the lobby and looked for signs for the Clifton School Reunion. Not seeing any, I asked the receptionist, who peered somewhat disgustedly through her glasses at me and pointed to a door that clearly said 'Clifton School Reunion'.

'Oops. Silly me. Sorry,' I said guiltily as she totally ignored me.

I hobbled towards it. Unfortunately, someone pulled the door open at the exact same time I tried to push it. I fell through and landed with a loud thud down three steps into the garden party. I really should have practised walking with crutches a little more. Why oh why was I so damn clumsy all the time? I read somewhere once that women are more accident-prone when they have their periods. It must be true for me, at least.

Wanting so desperately for the floor to open up and engulf me, as I had flashbacks to my inelegant fall at work, I slowly lifted my head to see about fifty people all staring at me. I wanted to cry. Iso wanted to cry. But that would make me look even more stupid, so I laughed instead. In fact, I laughed hysterically, so hysterically that people stopped feeling sorry for the great oaf tangled up in a mess on the floor and began laughing too. Laughing at me, not with me. But, nevertheless, they were laughing. I'm sure I'd made a great conversation point for everyone, anyway.

Suddenly I heard a shriek that slightly resembled a cat being trapped in the door. I knew that sound because I'd accidentally been the cause of it at a friend's house when I was about five. I hadn't known the bloody cat slept in the doorway, had I?

'Eeeeeek. It's Summer. Summer Miller!' A little fat woman bounded towards me with quite a handsome but older man in tow.

'Summer! Goodness me. Are you alright? Here let me help you. Oh dear. You've obviously been making these falls quite a regular occurrence by the looks of that leg. Hang on, there we go. Are you alright?'

She and her handsome companion helped me up while I dusted myself down, trying hard to figure out who she was. It was no good, I didn't have a clue.

I mumbled something like, 'Thanks ever so much…?' and she shrieked and giggled.

'You don't recognise me, do you?'

Looking slightly embarrassed, I shook my head.

'It's me. Samantha Bartson, although I'm not Bartson anymore. I'm Smith.'

What? This little chubby thing was Samantha Bartson the Tartson? My God. What on Earth had happened to her? She used to be the school's easiest lay. Back then she'd been slim, sexy and very attractive and took full advantage of it. I never liked her much, although I pretended to. I was jealous as hell. She had been a very early developer. In fact, if I remember correctly, she had huge boobs when she was twelve. I didn't have anything till I was sixteen. But now...Jesus. It was very hard to believe.

'Samantha! Wow. You look absolutely terrific,' I lied.

She giggled and blushed and suddenly remembered to introduce the attractive man at her side, 'Ooh, I'm sorry. This is Damian Smith, my husband. Damian, this is Summer, one of my oldest friends,' I felt a stab of guilt, which lasted all of a second. She was married to this hunk? God, life wasn't fair. It really wasn't damn fair.

I shook his hand, and he winked at me. 'Pleasure to meet you, Summer,' he said with a very posh English accent.

Samantha was rummaging around in her handbag and mumbling on about God knows what. '... and they're so lovely. Do you have any? Oh, I guess not. You're all on your own. Here we are. This is Tara. She's four. This is Danny, who's also four. They're twins. This here is Nicky, and he's just turned two, and finally, here is Becky, who's just turned eight months!'

Bloody hell! Well, she'd been busy since school. I nodded and smiled, muttering something about how lovely they all were. I was dying to ask if they all had the same father, but thought better of it, although her comment about my being alone was a bit below the belt. Maybe I should have asked her. Fortunately, I didn't have to engage in further chit-chat because I was rescued.

'Summer!'

I turned and saw my oldest school friend, Jemma.

'Jemma!' I screamed back. Quickly excusing myself from the master of reproduction here, I hobbled over to her as quickly as I could.

'My God, Jemma. You look absolutely gorgeous!' I was honest

this time. 'I thought you'd moved to Australia with Matt?' Matt had been her high school sweetheart.

We hugged each other, and she told me she had. 'I still live there with him. I didn't want to miss this for the world. I lost your address a few years ago, too, and you're not on Facebook or anything, so this was the perfect opportunity to catch up. How are you? Not too good by the looks of things.'

'Oh, this. This is nothing. I was run over by Madonna's body-guards in Hyde Park while out jogging.'

Her face dropped. 'Oh, you poor thing.'

I pointed and laughed. 'Jemma, you've obviously not changed a bit. You're still as gullible as ever. I fell over at work, down some stairs.'

'And you're exactly the same too,' she said, as she playfully punched my shoulder.

'So where is Matt then?'

'He couldn't come. He's too busy at the farm back home.'

'You have a farm?' I couldn't quite picture her with wellies and pigs and cows and stuff.

But she nodded. 'I know it's crazy, isn't it? But it's made us quite a bit of money. It's doing really well, and we're happy. That's what's important, isn't it? Tell me about you? What have you been up to?'

A waiter approached us with champagne, which we gratefully took and sipped as I told her about my new job and the disastrous men in my life up until that point.

'Don't worry, Summer. You'll find someone right for you soon. All the others just weren't meant to be.'

'Enough about me. What the hell happened to Samantha?' I asked as we both sneaked a look at her and laughed.

'Too much sex. Have you seen the number of kids she's got?'

We chatted for another hour or so, drinking more champagne until we were distracted by a commotion near the front of the garden. Wondering what all the fuss was about, we stood up to go and have a look. That was when I noticed people looking at me rather oddly.

Oh shit, was my dress tucked in my knickers? Did I have the remains of a mushroom vol-au-vent stuck to my chin or something? I asked Jemma, and she said there was nothing wrong with me, but she obviously cottoned on to it, whatever it was, and grinned at me too, as she moved out from in front of me to reveal a massive truck in the road near the garden. On it were six words.

Summer Miller, Will You Be Mine?

CHAPTER 18

$\mathcal{J}$ was totally gobsmacked.

There was no-one from school who would want me. There was no-one from school who I'd want, for that matter. God, was this some kind of sick joke or something? I looked around to see if I could recognise any of the men, but all the men there had women with them. People were staring at me, grinning, almost cheering me on.

I smiled back shyly, not knowing quite what to say.

Jemma stood by my side, 'So, who did this, then? Is there a man you didn't tell me about?' She gasped. 'You're not being stalked, are you? I read about a girl who was stalked by a guy for years, and she didn't know about it. He finally showed his face and proposed. Of course, she said no. She didn't even know the guy. Days later, her body was found...without its head. Creepy, eh? He must have kept it for a souvenir. Maybe he kissed it goodnight every night before he went to bed. Come to think of it, I don't think they ever found him or her head.'

'Thanks, Jemma. That was just what I needed,' I said sarcastically, as I nudged her in the stomach.

Then I saw him.

And I fainted.

oOo

I CAME to about ten minutes later, apparently. I was lying on a garden chaise-longue. My initial thought was, 'this doesn't belong to me, but it's rather nice. I wonder if I'd get away with taking it home'. A strange thought, I know, but a peculiar situation, right?

My eyes slowly came into focus, and kneeling beside me was Jemma. Jemma from school. 'Jemma. I haven't seen you for years. What on Earth are you doing here?' I asked slowly.

She smiled at me and explained where we were. But I just shook my head and mumbled, 'No I didn't come to any school reunion. What are you talking about?'

'She's clearly disorientated, do you think we should take her to the hospital?' said a voice above me.

But the word 'hospital' brought me back to reality, and I sat bolt upright, shaking my head. 'Nobody is taking me to the hospital. Whatever happened? I'm fine. What did happen, anyway?'

'Don't you remember the truck?'

I shook my head.

'The words on the truck?'

'What? I was on a truck with words? Huh?'

Jemma shook her head and explained what had happened. '... then you passed out. This gorgeous guy climbed out of the truck and ran over to you. I think he went inside the hotel to get you some sweet tea or something.'

It all came back to me. It was Ryan. My darling sweet Ryan had come for me.

I stood up, forgetting, once again, about my cast, and plonked straight back down again. Shit. Then I heard the most amazing, sexy voice say, 'Has she come to, yet? Is she okay?'

I turned and came face to face with the man of my dreams. Dreams? Oh Shit. I was dreaming again. This was so bloody typical. My hopes would be shattered once again by my alarm clock. I looked away from the inexistent Ryan and lay back down. I figured I may as well lie down until I woke up.

'Summer? Summer? Are you alright?' asked Ryan and Jemma together.

I ignored them. It was pointless talking to imaginary people. So I sat in silence, waiting for that dreaded moment: morning.

After a while, nothing seemed to happen, except for Ryan trying to make me drink tea with Jemma sitting beside me, continuously asking if I was alright.

Suddenly I heard a shriek of laughter. It sounded distinctly like Samantha Bartson the Tartson. Why the hell would she be in my dream? I certainly wouldn't put her there. Then I realised maybe it really wasn't a dream. Perhaps this was reality. Ryan was here... and he wants me to be his girl, and I'd been dissing him as if he didn't exist. I decided to pinch myself. Ouch!

I asked Jemma to pinch me too. Double ouch! Then I asked Ryan to pinch me, ...and he planted the most amazing kiss on my lips.

'Oh, Ryan, I thought I was dreaming. I've dreamed so much about you since Portugal. I've missed you so much!'

Suddenly there was a massive round of applause, and I realised we had an audience. In fact, the whole reunion seemed to be taking part around us. I blushed crimson and hid my face in Ryan's arms.

'I've missed you too, but... But you haven't answered me?' he said in those dulcet American tones.

'What do you mean?'

He pointed to the truck across the street and got down on one knee. 'Summer, I really missed you since we split in Portugal. I've thought about nothing else but you. I've been completely miserable. I know we were only together for a few weeks, but that means nothing when two people are meant to be together. I love you so much, and I want to be with you for the rest of my life. Will you...will you give me another chance?'

I cried so much that my mascara covered my cheeks. I must have looked gorgeous. And then, finally, I answered him.

'Ryan. Of course, I will... but can we take it slowly?'

Ryan let his head drop backwards, and he closed his eyes, a

massive grin spreading across his cheeks before he nodded. 'Of course we can, baby. I love you.'

He helped me stand up, and we embraced each other and kissed as everyone clapped and cheered around us.

At that moment, I was the happiest girl in the world, but there was something I was confused about. How had he known where to find me? I had to ask.

He smiled his sexy Ryan-smile, and his eyes twinkled as he spoke. 'Gwen told me.'

I must have looked confused because he continued. 'She and Hugh decided to go to Houston for part of their honeymoon, and they got in touch with Brad. They told him you'd been totally miserable and he told them so had I, so we all met up and arranged what to do about it.' He grinned.

'So Gwen knows all about this?' I asked happily.

He nodded. 'When she called you earlier in the week, she knew I'd already booked a flight, but she wanted to keep it a surprise. The real reason she called was to find out where you would be today. Oh, and by the way, I love the hair,' he grinned, showing off those beautiful slightly wonky white teeth. I just loved those teeth.

But Gwen. What a darling. What a pal. I couldn't believe it.

I sighed with pure blissful happiness as I leaned forward and kissed the man who had suddenly brought so much joy to my life.

Arm in arm, we hobbled towards the truck.

'Your place or mine?' he whispered.

'Today, mine. Tomorrow, maybe yours. Who knows?' I replied, as I cheekily pinched his bum.

EPILOGUE

A cute gurgling sound came out of the crib next to the Christmas tree.

'Awww, she's laughing again,' I said, leaning over the darling little thing all wrapped up neatly in her bed.

'Huh? No, honey, she's doing a poo,' Gwen said, yawning.

'Oh, lovely,' I cringed inching away from the subtle aroma delicately hovering in the air.

'Hugh darling? The baby's bum needs changing.'

Gwen winked at me as we both watched him come rushing into the living room, breathlessly carrying everything needed to clean up his little Angel's bottom.

'Wow, you're right. It is amazing,' I laughed.

'What? What's amazing?' Hugh asked absent-mindedly as he proceeded to lift little Amelia out of the crib.

'How quickly you come running to tend to your daughter,' I replied with a chuckle. 'You really are quite the doting dad, aren't you?'

Hugh's cheeks blushed, and he grinned.

'You don't need to say a thing. I can see it for myself, and it's bloody wonderful, Hugh. Gwen, you're one lucky lady.'

Gwen squeezed my shoulder while looking proudly at her new family, 'I know,' she whispered before yawning again. 'But it's tiring, being a mum.'

'You're doing a great job, Gwen. Even though you have to get up every few hours to feed her, you're looking amazing.'

'Aww thanks, hon,' she smiled. 'Where's Ryan?'

'I'm right here,' yelled a voice coming from the kitchen before he appeared in the doorway carrying a tray containing three glasses and a mug.

'Three mulled ciders for those of us who can,' he winked at me, making my legs go weak at the knees. 'And a special cinnamon hot chocolate for the lady who's breastfeeding,' he said, handing each of us a drink.

'Ryan, you're totally awesome,' Gwen laughed.

'Glad to hear some of my Americanisms are rubbing off on you.'

'All clean,' said Hugh as he held his little three-week-old 'cherry-pie' up to his face for a kiss before he lovingly placed her back down for more sleep.

Ryan handed him his drink before lifting his own, 'Cheers, mate.'

Hugh laughed, 'Glad to hear some of our Englishisms are rubbing off on you too. Cheers.'

As we all sat down, my mum appeared wearing one of those awful naked aprons, wielding a glass of mulled cider in one hand and a plate full of pigs in blankets in the other.

'Anyone for a pig in blanket?' she grinned.

'Oooh yes please, Miss M,' said Gwen, 'I'm starving.'

'Well, lunch won't be served for a good few hours yet, Gwen sweetheart so dig in. I'll leave them on the coffee table.'

As she put them down, the doorbell rang. Mum shot upright and blushed. Her hand instinctively going to her hair.

'You look beautiful, Mum,' I said proudly as I stood to go and let Jack in. He'd been away for a few days, and she was clearly missing him.

'I'll just pop upstairs to check my face,' she said, quickly disappearing.

Out in the hallway of Hugh's huge house, I opened the door.

'Hi, Jack.'

'Summer!' he exclaimed happily. 'Merry Christmas!'

'Merry Christmas to you too. I'm delighted you're here. Mum's just popped upstairs. She'll be down in a sec.'

Jack stepped inside, carrying a couple of huge Father Christmas style sacks which he carefully placed on the floor before pulling me in for a quick hug and a peck on the cheek.

'I appreciate the invitation, Summer. It was kind of you, Hugh and Gwen to invite your mum and me.'

'Are you kidding? You're family now, Jack. I feel like I should start calling you Dad or something,' I chuckled as I watched him redden slightly. I couldn't help notice a look of pride appear on his face, though, before he grinned again and nodded. 'It's really something else to feel wanted. Thank you.'

I hugged him quickly and shooed him into the living room where everyone made him feel extra welcome, while I headed upstairs to see what was taking Mum so long.

'Mum?'

'Summer? Erm, just a sec.'

'Where are you?'

'Hang on.'

I stood on the landing and waited, patiently, for a couple of minutes before she appeared from one of the spare bedrooms carrying something small in her hands and her handbag in the other.

'Are you alright?' I asked.

She smiled, 'I was just wrapping this. I didn't get the chance to do it properly before now.'

She handed me a little box, carefully wrapped in silver and purple paper, with a pink bow around it.

'But you already gave me my Christmas present, Mum. You didn't have to get me something else.'

'I wanted to. Here. Open it.'

I could feel the smile spread across my cheeks as I very carefully undid the bow and peeled back the tape. Before I opened the box, I looked up at her. Mum had changed so much in the last few months. Her relationship with Jack had blossomed so much, and she was incredibly happy that her skin had changed, her hair too.

She looked younger than ever actually, and I was only just noticing
it.

'I love you, Mum,' I whispered.

'I know, my Angel. I love you too. Now open it.'

Grinning again, I opened the box. Inside was an exquisite,
exotic-looking gold ring.

'Oh, Mum, it's stunning.'

She smiled, 'Jack and I got it in India last month. I saw it and
just knew it was perfect for you. Look, I even had it engraved.'

On closer inspection, I saw the words, A Special Summer.

'Aww Mum, I absolutely love it. Thank you so much.'

'There's something else too,' she said, her eyes super wide as she
reached into her handbag, retrieving an envelope and handing it
to me.

'Jack and I have been doing some 'investigating', and we found
him, Summer.'

I stumbled backwards slightly. 'Found who?' I whispered, even
though I already knew the answer.

'Tristan. We found your dad.'

I swallowed loudly.

'It wasn't fair what I did to you,' she said, shaking her head. 'I
should never have lied to you about your father, and I regret it so
badly, Summer. Hopefully now–but only if you really want to–you
can contact him yourself and find out everything you ever wanted
to know. This envelope contains his name, telephone number,
address and email.'

I could feel the tears welling up in the corners of my eyes as I
looked down at her sad face. I leaned forward and hugged her
tight.

'Thanks, Mum. This means the world to me.'

'I hope so, sweetie. I really do. I know that you're moving
upwards and onwards with your life right now Summer and I
didn't want you to have doubts about who you are anymore. Plus, I
have a feeling you'll be making a family of your own quite soon
with that hunk of a man you've got,' she chuckled, sniffing at the
same time.

'Hey, what's going on up here,' said that sexy voice as Ryan appeared up the stairs. 'Are my girls crying? Why are you crying?"

Mum pulled away from me and readjusted a few strands of long blonde hair from my face before turning to Ryan.

'Happy tears, sunshine,' she smiled. 'Just happy tears. Right, I'm going to check on lunch,' she said, carefully wiping her eyes before plastering on a big smile and heading back downstairs to the party.

'What's going on, babe?' Ryan asked as he took me into his comforting arms, making (as usual) my knees go weak.

Smiling, I planted my hands firmly on his bum and squeezed, 'I'm just really, really happy right now, and it's mostly because of you.'

'Only mostly?' he smirked.

'Well, almost entirely... but I have a lot to do with it too. As well as my mum, and work, and Jack, and Gwen, and Hugh and of course little Amelia. But mostly you.'

He grinned, and I melted into him as his lips met mine in the most passionate kiss. When we pulled apart for air, we both giggled at each other.

'You remember when I told you I wanted to take it slow?'

He nodded, his head dropping to one side.

'I'm ready to speed it up now.'

I watched as his nostrils flared slightly and he gulped before he narrowed his eyes with a cheeky grin, 'how fast do you wanna go, sugar?'

'How about hyperdrive?'

Ryan's laughter made me jump.

'Hyperdrive?'

I nodded, trying to look serious.

'Faster than the speed of light?' he asked.

I started laughing with him, 'Absolutely.'

'Then what are we waiting for? Baby, are you ready for this?'

'I've never been more ready for anything in my life. Let's do it...'

THE END

ABOUT THE AUTHOR

Suzy Turner wrote her first chick lit novel in her early twenties, but it wasn't until much later that she decided to focus on writing full time. It was during a visit to Canada in 2009 when the ravens within the dark eerie forests of British Columbia called to her. The story of Lilly Taylor was born soon after and the first novel in The Raven Witch Saga was created. Suzy has since published several more urban fantasy books (under her pen name SG Turner) and contemporary women's novels.

Having lived in Portugal since childhood, Suzy, who is originally from Yorkshire in England, loves to travel. She finds inspiration wherever she goes. Old decrepit buildings, graveyards, cathedrals and castles are just a few of the things that can be found within the worlds of her urban fantasy books, and her contemporary women's fiction novels are filled with fun friendships, ordinary people in extraordinary circumstances and quirky characters you'd want as friends.

Suzy lives in the Algarve with her husband, three cats and a dog, where she does yoga every morning and bookish stuff for pretty much the rest of the day!

For more books and updates, visit www.suzyturner.com

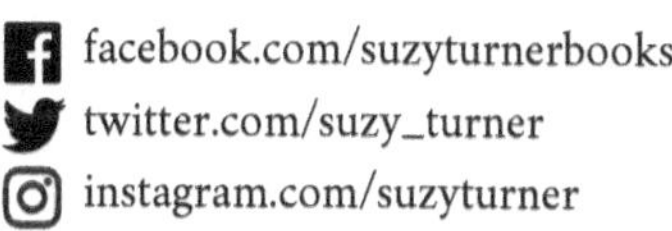

ACKNOWLEDGMENTS

I wrote this book in my mid-twenties. It was my very first attempt at writing a novel. Admittedly, I was amazed I could do it! But after various failed attempts at getting an agent, I gave up, put the book in a drawer somewhere and pretty much forgot all about it... until recently when, after writing nine other novels, I decided it was time to dust it off, clean it up and share it with the world!

I'm very grateful to the wonderful girls who read this first and gave me their honest opinions to help hone Stormy Summer into an even better book.
– Christine, Jill, Poppet, Dawn, Lorna –
You girls rock!
Huge thanks should also go to my awesome editor, Andrea, who works magic on my books, every single time.
And last but certainly not least, to my very own knight in shining armour, Michael,
who has been with me from the very beginning of my journey – helping me every
step of the way (even though he still hasn't read any of my books – he insists he's waiting for the movies!).